THE THREE MUSKETEERS

Alexandre Dumas

Om
KIDZ

An imprint of Om Books International

Reprinted in 2016

Om KIDZ

An imprint of Om Books International

Corporate & Editorial Office
A-12, Sector 64, Noida 201 301
Uttar Pradesh, India
Phone: +91 120 477 4100
Email: editorial@ombooks.com
Website: www.ombooksinternational.com

Sales Office
107, Ansari Road, Darya Ganj
New Delhi 110 002, India
Phone: +91 11 4000 9000
Fax: +91 11 2327 8091
Email: sales@ombooks.com
Website: www.ombooks.com

Adapted by Subhojit Sanyal
Illustrated by Aadil Khan, Manoj Kumar Prasad

ISBN: 978-93-81607-47-3

Printed in India

10 9 8 7 6 5 4 3

Contents

Chapter One

The Man from Gascony

The citizens of Meung, a small French town, were quite amazed that bright April morning. It was the year 1625 and they all left whatever they were doing just to stare at what they saw before them. A young man came riding into the village, on a horse so old and lean that the poor creature seeemed to hang its head low in embarrassment. Its coat had all but disappeared, leaving only a slight orange hint of fur, and its tail was absolutely devoid of any hair. The villagers stared at each other and nodded their heads, agreeing silently that the man they were seeing before them had to be from Gascony, the only place in the entire country where a person would have the courage to ride a nag like that and be proud of it.

And they were indeed right, because young D'artagnan was unbelievably happy that day. He was set for a long journey, one that would take him all the way to France. He was soon going to join the illustrious Musketeers, the brave and fearless men who took pride in serving and securing the royal person of the King of France, King Louis XIII.

D'artagnan ran his hands through his pockets to check whether he had the three things which his father had given him when he had started off for Paris. One was a small bag that contained fifteen hundred gold crowns, a rather sizeable amount to begin a new life in a distant city. The second was a sword that had been in the family for many generations and D'artagnan felt a great amount of pride in being able to wield it effectively. In addition, there was also a letter from his father for Monsieur de Tréville, the Captain of the King's Musketeers.

As D'artagnan led his horse through the village, he could hear his father's words ringing in his ears. "I have taught you all that I could, my son. But always remember, I have taught you to use the

sword and you have learnt how to use it well. So never walk away from a fight, however daunting your opponent might be. Never forget the fact that you are a Gascon, you are fearless and also that you are my son."

It was quite late in the day, when D'artagnan finally arrived at his destination, the inn in Meung. But even before he could get off his horse and walk into the inn, he saw three men standing there, laughing uncontrollably. D'artagnan did not mind their mirth at first, but the men then turned around and kept staring at him and his horse and continued to laugh even harder.

D'artagnan jumped off his horse and very calmly asked, "If I may, Sir, could I know the reason behind your laughter? If I do find it amusing, I wouldn't mind laughing along with you fine gentlemen."

This just made the men laugh even more. One of them, a tall nobleman wearing a black coat with a black patch over one of his eyes and a scar on his cheek, turned to D'artagnan with a smile, but said nothing. He simply pointed at D'artagnan's horse and laughed even more. The other two gentlemen who were standing with the nobleman too broke into peals of laughter.

"If you laugh at my horse, then you must know this, Sir, that you really laugh at me!" cried D'artagnan, losing his temper slightly.

The nobleman looked back at him once again and gently replied, "I do not think that I am talking to you, young man!"

"But Sir, I am indeed talking to you and no one else. You have laughed at my horse for quite some time, now perhaps you would prefer laughing at the owner of that horse!" and so saying, D'artagnan took his sword out of its sheath and waved it before the three men.

The nobleman merely smiled and immediately turned around to go back into the inn. D'artagnan would have nothing of it, and he ran straight for the nobleman, yelling, "Turn around and face me like a man, or lose your life with a single blow of my sword!".

At this, the nobleman spun around on his heels and snapped his sword out. His smile had vanished as he clenched his teeth and looked at D'artagnan. But the duel never started, since one of the nobleman's friends struck D'artagnan from behind with a shovel, making him unconscious.

As the young Gascon lay there, blood oozing out of the injury he sustained to his head, the innkeeper sent out two of his men to bring D'artagnan inside. As he was being made to lie down on a bed after his head was bandaged, an envelope dropped out of D'artagnan's pocket. The innkeeper bent down and picked it up at once, and without a second thought he tore open the envelope and started reading its contents.

"Hmm!" exclaimed the innkeeper, "A letter for the Captain of the Musketeers! Most interesting... I am sure the nobleman outside will be very interested in this." And the innkeeper rushed out at once.

And indeed! The nobleman was rather curious on receiving the letter from the innkeeper. "What business does that young fool have with my enemy?" he muttered to himself. "I'll have to deal

with this later. Right now it is absolutely imperative that I finish my business with Milady or it might be too late!"

D'artagnan was starting to come around. His head was still reeling from the blow he had received, but he managed to drag himself off the bed and started to walk towards the window. He saw a fancy carriage pull up next to the inn and a beautiful lady put her head out of the window, looking for someone. D'artagnan saw the nobleman who had laughed at him walk up to the carriage. He strained his ears and heard the nobleman tell the lady, "He has asked you to leave for London at once. The Cardinal insists that you spend as much time as you can in the court and keep reporting to him on the Duke's every move. And be careful, the Cardinal fears Buckingham may be leaving London. Make sure that you learn about that beforehand."

The lady smiled at the nobleman and replied, "Don't worry, I'll be successful in my mission. But you too must be on your way. We wouldn't want any delays now with interfering young men. The Cardinal will be most cross."

D'artagnan could only stand there in shock. He was certain that the two of them were discussing important matters of state. Cardinal Richelieu, after all, was the most powerful man in the whole of France and it was believed that it was actually the Cardinal who ruled over the country. And D'artagnan could also make out that they had been talking about the Duke of Buckingham, the Prime Minister of England, the man who was the real strength behind the rule of King Charles I.

But before D'artagnan could do anything, the nobleman sprang on to his horse and rode away very quickly. The young Gascon yelled from the window, "Come back here, you wretch! And face me like a man..." However, it was too late. He was already out of sight and D'artagnan was too weak at the time to chase him.

As D'artagnan slipped into his bed, he wondered what the nobleman and the lady were talking of. The lady was no doubt a spy, who was being sent to London at the Cardinal's behest to monitor the Prime Minister of England. Some major political upheaval was surely in the offing!

As D'artagnan was getting ready to resume his journey to Paris the next day, he noticed that his introduction letter to Monsieur de Tréville was missing. He rushed out at once and grabbed the innkeeper by the collar, yelling, "My letter! What have you done with it? Where have you taken it? Give it back right now, or else I will cut your head off with my sword!"

The frightened innkeeper folded his hands before D'artagnan and pleaded, "I don't know anything about any letter, Sir... Maybe it was that nobleman from yesterday, perhaps he took it!"

D'artagnan was furious. "He has not seen the end of this," he said to himself. He walked out of the inn and mounting his horse, started off towards Paris at once. "Monsieur de Tréville will definitely help me find that horrible man. I will have my justice yet!"

Chapter Two

The King's Musketeers

The clamour outside was enthralling. D'artagnan could not believe that he was finally standing in the courtyard of Monsieur de Tréville, the Captain of the King's Musketeers. All the musketeers were standing before him, fighting mock duels, chatting with each other and, of course, many of them were cracking jokes at the expense of the Cardinal's Guards, who, although not overtly, were their enemies.

D'artagnan was wonderstruck as he walked through the mêlée and arrived at a large door. It was the building where the Captain of the Musketeers, Monsieur de Tréville had his offices. D'artagnan asked the soldier on guard at the door to inform the Captain about him. Within minutes, the Captain himself was at the door. As he ordered D'artagnan to walk up to his office, he pushed his head outside and screamed, "Athos, Porthos, Aramis!"

D'artagnan maintained his respect for the Captain of the Musketeers and stood quietly inside the door, waiting to follow the Captain to his office. He could see two of the men standing at the courtyard leave at once on hearing the Captain's call. Soon, D'artagnan was standing in Monsieur de Tréville's office with the two Musketeers.

"What do you all have to say for yourselves? Is this the behaviour expected from one of the King's own Musketeers? And don't deny it... the Cardinal's guards recognised all three of you. Just imagine that! Starting a brawl like that in front of a wine shop and then getting caught in the act too! Do you fine gentlemen have no respect for the title you bear?" Monsieur de Tréville was irate. He never liked reports against his Musketeers from the Cardinal's guards.

Porthos slowly started, "But Sir, you have just heard..."

But Monsieur de Tréville was in no mood to listen to their excuses. Instead, he interrupted Porthos from speaking any further and asked, "I just see two of you here. I distinctly remember asking Athos to come here too! Where on earth is he?"

"But Sir, that's what I was trying to tell you... Athos is not very well, Sir!" Porthos spoke gently, quite scared of his Captain's tirade.

Aramis too added, "I would not say that he is unwell, Sir, as much as he is wounded. The Cardinal's guards did not give you a very true account of what had happened there that day."

Monsieur de Tréville's expression changed from that of rage to compassion. "Why? What happened then? Speak freely, my Musketeers!"

Just as Porthos was about to speak again, the door flung wide open and a wounded Musketeer came charging into the room, his face contorted with pain, and D'artagnan guessed the new Musketeer was Athos.

"Sir, I believe you called me..." Athos began, his voice rather weak.

Monsieur de Tréville came forward and grabbed Athos by his shoulders. "My goodness, what has happened to you, Athos?"

Porthos then spoke again, as he turned towards Athos and said, "There were six of them, Sir, and only the three of us. However, we maintained the honour of the Musketeers and fought rather well with them. Athos, though, was wounded while exchanging blows, as you can perhaps see for yourself!"

Monsieur de Tréville smiled as he looked at all the three Musketeers standing before him. "I must say that all of you have indeed shown great courage in the face of such adversity, and I am indeed proud of you men. But you were lucky this time, particularly you, Athos. I don't want a similar incident to happen again."

The Musketeers were dismissed by the Captain, as he turned to D'artagnan and said, "Your father is one of my oldest friends... Please, tell me what I can do for you here in Paris!"

D'artagnan was still a little fazed by what he had just witnessed and very meekly, he replied,

"Sir, my father sent me all the way here to become a part of the King's Musketeers. But now I feel that I am not suitable to stand next to these valiant men."

Monsieur de Tréville smiled, happy on hearing D'artagnan's words. But shaking his head, the Captain replied, "My son, I regret to inform you that you can only become a part of the King's Musketeers if you have already committed some rather bold task, or at least served in the lower regiments of the King's army and attained sufficient skill and training in wielding weapons."

D'artagnan smiled and replied respectfully, "Sir, forgive me for speaking thus, but I had with me a letter from my father which could have explained my prowess to you. But alas, the letter was stolen from me during my journey here."

D'artagnan then went on to tell Monsieur de Tréville all that happened at the inn in Meung. As he spoke of the nobleman with the eye patch and scar on his cheek, Monsieur de Tréville started to get visibly upset.

"Are you absolutely sure about this nobleman?" Monsieur de Tréville asked D'artagnan as he finished his tale.

D'artagnan honestly replied, "Why yes Sir! How could I make a mistake... I remember his features very clearly."

"And are you sure you heard him speak to this lady you mention? He called her Milady, are you sure of that?" Monsieur de Tréville insisted.

"Absolutely, Sir! I was right there, listening to them from the window above," D'artagnan confidently said to the Captain.

"Oh mon dieu! Then it is true... he is back and Milady is off to England right now, plotting against the Duke of Buckingham!" Monsieur de Tréville cried out softly.

D'artagnan jumped on seeing the Captain's reaction. He bent over the table and said excitedly, "Do you know the man, Sir? In which case you must tell me his name and where I can find him... I must get my revenge. He has not seen the last of me yet!"

But Monsieur de Tréville would have nothing of it. "Most certainly not! Get these silly ideas out of your head. Forget him and never even think of entering into a fight with him. He has friends in extremely influential positions. Now sit here

quietly, while I write a letter of recommendation to one of the lower regiments I just mentioned. Serve your time as a cadet first and then you can become a part of the King's Musketeers."

As Monsieur de Tréville got busy writing that letter, D'artagnan paced around the room, mulling over the words that the Captain had just told him about the nobleman. As he went across to the window, he saw something far in the distance and the young Gascon at once got extremely agitated.

He rushed out of the office without another word, screaming, "Not again, not again, not again!"

Monsieur de Tréville did not even have any time to understand what was happening. As D'artagnan slipped through the door, Monsieur de Tréville cried out after him, "What happened? Who did you see?"

"My enemy, the man from Meung!" and the young man was gone from there in a flash.

Chapter Three

Fighting the Musketeers

D'artagnan rushed out of Monsieur de Tréville's office like a man possessed. He was so filled with rage, anger and the humiliation that he had suffered by deceit at Meung that he did not see a Musketeer standing at the landing before the main door and ran straight into him. D'artagnan tried to find a way past the Musketeer after having hit him with his entire body, but the Musketeer too would have none of it and kept blocking any route that D'artagnan would choose to get by him.

"You seem to be in one big hurry," said the Musketeer rather curtly.

In no mood to talk to a Musketeer at that moment, D'artagnan came back saying, "It is best for you to move out of my way!"

29

"Oh is it now?" the Musketeer asked, rather amused at D'artagnan's gutsy reply. D'artagnan too realised that it would perhaps benefit him more to stop and exchange a few words with the Musketeer, instead of trying to find a way past the elite warrior. As soon as he stopped and faced the Musketeer, D'artagnan's face dropped. It was Athos.

"Oh you must forgive me, my lord, for hurting your wounds. Please accept my word that I did not intend to purposefully cause you any more harm," D'artagnan said with genuine respect.

But Athos obviously was not impressed with his words, particularly after the way in which he was behaving just a few moments back. "I do not think I can believe you because clearly you are one with no manners!" Athos exclaimed.

"For someone who started a fight with the Cardinal's guards, I do not think that you are in any position to give me a speech on manners and etiquette," said D'artagnan, upset at the prospect of not being able to chase the nobleman from Meung.

Athos smiled, amazed at the courage with which D'artagnan was speaking to him and said, "If not in manners, I think I can teach you something about duelling then!"

D'artagnan remembered his father's words about walking away from a fight and knowing fully well that Athos was a King's Musketeer, he replied, "I accept your challenge. Tell me when and where we must have this duel and I shall be there, waiting for you."

"Then we shall meet again today, at noon, behind the Carmelite Convent, and we shall settle our scores as gentlemen there," Athos declared, as he stepped away and let D'artagnan pass.

D'artagnan was aware of the time he had lost in arguing with Athos and he tried to make up for lost time by running in the direction he had seen the nobleman from Meung go. As he reached the gates of the courtyard, he saw Porthos standing there, in conversation with another Musketeer. D'artagnan judged that there was indeed enough space for him to pass through and started running towards the gate.

However, just as he was about to run past Porthos and his friend, the wind picked up all of a sudden and D'artagnan was caught in Porthos' cloak. He tried to wriggle his way through the cloak of the burly Musketeer, but was completely trapped in the heavy cloth.

Porthos pulled his cloak aside and found D'artagnan straddled within the little space between him and the gate. Looking quite cross, he said, "Only madmen rush without looking through their eyes, and you, therefore need to be treated in the same way as a lunatic."

D'artagnan was already feeling quite helpless about not being able to run after the nobleman and he retorted, "And you Sir, are going to rid me of my madness?"

Porthos was not pleased one bit with D'artagnan's lack of respect and he scoffed, "Yes indeed, Sir, I am. I shall be ready for you at one behind the Luxembourg Gardens. Be there or believe me, I shall hunt you down."

"I shall be there, even if it takes my life," replied D'artagnan and sped away from there.

He ran through almost all the streets and alleys of Paris, yet he had no luck in sighting even the slightest trace of the nobleman from Meung. As he turned away, disappointed, D'artagnan thought back on the events that had just unfolded in his life. He had lost the letter his father had written for Monsieur de Tréville to a nobleman in Meung, he had made a bad impression on Monsieur de Tréville again when he rushed out of his office without even requesting his permission and finally, he had landed two duels for himself, each with one of the King's Musketeers. "What have I done? They are Musketeers and can kill me in just a few seconds! If I do survive today, I must be more careful in the future!" D'artagnan consoled himself.

As he started making his way to the Carmelite Convent to keep his appointment with Athos, he saw the third Musketeer he had seen that morning in Monsieur de Tréville's office, Aramis, standing before him, talking to some of his friends.

D'artagnan thought it best to seek his path away from the third Musketeer, but suddenly he saw Aramis drop his handkerchief and step on it.

After his previous experiences with the Musketeers, D'artagnan felt this was an opportunity for him to start mending his ways. Therefore, without wasting any time, he walked over hurriedly to were Aramis and his Musketeer friends were standing and, pulling the handkerchief from under his shoes, politely said, "Excuse me, Sir, but I believe you dropped this..."

Aramis looked at D'artagnan, his face flushed with puzzlement and surprise. He was in absolute shock and embarrassed, as his friends started hooting, "Ah ha! A perfumed lace handkerchief and that too one which Aramis was trying to hide? Come, dear friend, tell us all about her! I'm rather sure this belongs to one of the Queen's ladies-in-waiting."

Aramis tried to hide his embarrassment from his friends, but turning to D'artagnan, he exclaimed, "Have you no manners at all? Do you not have even the basic etiquette to understand that if a man is stepping on a woman's handkerchief, he is trying to hide something?"

"I am sorry Sir," D'artagnan began, "I was completely unaware…"

But Aramis would have nothing of it. He rudely interrupted D'artagnan and angrily declared, "Your callous act does not deserve any forgiveness! You are but a village fool!"

D'artagnan did not obviously take too kindly to Aramis' harsh words and retorted, "You are in no position to dictate manners to me, Sir!"

"I won't," agreed Aramis, "but my sword will. Be ready at two behind the Church and we shall sort this out as gentlemen do."

"You will find me exactly where you ask," replied D'artagnan adamantly. Since he was already late for his duel with Athos, D'artagnan bid a hasty farewell.

There was an vacant piece of land right behind the Carmelite Convent. As D'artagnan set across towards the plain land, he saw Athos already waiting for him on the other side. The fear of death gripped D'artagnan momentarily, but he consoled himself saying, "I know I have to die someday and I feel it is much better going at the hands of a Musketeer!"

Athos warmly welcomed D'artagnan and shaking his hand, the brave Musketeer said, "I hope you do not mind waiting for a while. My witnesses to this duel shall soon be arriving."

D'artagnan was impressed by the pleasant nature of Athos and therefore honestly confided in him, "I must admit Sir, I have no one here in Paris who will come along to stand witness in my fight. It was only today morning that I reached this great city and here I am, preparing to meet my death by afternoon. But I can die with honour, since I fight a Musketeer so brave, who dares to fight me even when wounded."

Athos bowed his head and creased a smile on his lips. He felt very grateful to D'artagnan for the great honour and mentioned, "The wounds do hurt, but I must bear them."

D'artagnan immediately offered, "Remind me later, if indeed it is possible, and I shall offer you a herbal remedy which is famous in Gascony!"

Athos laughed on hearing these words and stressed, "I am sure I will… for if we are not killed in this duel, then we shall surely be very good friends."

Athos broke off from D'artagnan as something else caught his eye. Two men, resembling the other Musketeers, were walking across the open field towards them. "Ah!" the Musketeer exclaimed, "Seems like my friends are here."

D'artagnan turned to the direction Athos was pointing towards and at once reacted in horror. "Porthos? Aramis? What are they doing here?"

"Why they are my closest friends. The whole of Paris knows us as the Three Musketeers. We live by our own motto, One for All, and All for One."

D'artagnan could not believe his own ears. He was so shocked that his mind could registered nothing Athos said anymore. "Good heavens, what is this lad doing here?" asked Porthos as soon as he was close enough.

Aramis too looked confused at D'artagnan's presence there. "Yes, this man has no business being here, particularly since I am to duel with him at two!" Aramis confessed.

Athos too, was now rather puzzled as to how D'artagnan had managed to get challenged by each of the Three Musketeers. Scratching his chin, he said, "Now that is quite an achievement, young man... you make dangerous enemies rather quickly!"

D'artagnan smiled innocently at Athos and drawing his sword, he said, "Now that you know how tied up I am, why don't we start the duel now, Monsieur Athos?"

Athos smiled slightly and nodded. He too dragged his sword out of the sheath and was ready to start the duel. But it had not even been a few moments since they started, that several of the Cardinal's Guards came running towards them.

Porthos yelled, "Stop with the fighting. Here come those dogs! They will surely try to make our lives miserable again."

But even before the Three Musketeers could do something, some of the Cardinal's Guards had already surrounded them. Aramis whispered to his friends, "I know there are five of them and only three of us, but I think we should still fight them off!"

Porthos agreed with Aramis' decision. "No way am I facing Monsieur de Tréville again after being defeated by the Cardinal's Guards."

Suddenly, a voice spoke out to the Three Musketeers. "I know that it is blasphemy even to consider myself one, but I do possess the heart and spirit of a Musketeer. Allow me to fight alongside you, and I swear that I shall make you proud!" D'artagnan said confidently.

"Well, there are five of them and three of us. Sure, you will be fighting alongside us, my good man!" Athos said with a shrug and together, the four of them unleashed themselves on the Cardinal's Guards.

D'artagnan fought like he had never fought before. He was living through the greatest dream of his entire life, that of fighting alongside the brave King's Musketeers. Within moments, they had killed four of the Cardinal's Guards and severely wounded the fifth Guard.

Athos signalled his friends to stop and declared, "I think we have more than made our point. This man cannot defend himself, so I suggest we take him towards the convent and leave him there."

The two other Musketeers and D'artagnan too, agreed with Athos and felt that it was the right

thing to do. The Three Musketeers then wrapped their arms around their new friend and started walking joyfully through the lanes of Paris. Just for fun, whenever they crossed someone, they all screamed in unison, "One for all, and all for one!"

No one was happier than D'artagnan at that point of time. He was actually singing and dancing with the Three Musketeers the very day he had arrived in Paris!

Chapter Four

Help Needed

Athos, Porthos, Aramis and also D'artagnan were once again standing in Monsieur de Tréville's office. The Captain of the Musketeers was saying, "I am sorry about having to be coarse with all of you down in the courtyard, but the illusion of our loyalty to the Cardinal must remain. I am proud of you, my men! You have been very brave to fight the Cardinal's Guards, particularly after you were outnumbered."

And the Captain was even more lavish in his praise for D'artagnan. "I knew that my friend's son would definitely be a brave and courageous lad. But what you have accomplished has surpassed my imagination completely."

King Louis XIII, too, congratulated the Three Musketeers and D'artagnan in private. It was true that Cardinal Richelieu had become the most powerful man in France because of the King's patronage and decrees, but Louis XIII even enjoyed Richelieu's embarrassment. He awarded D'artagnan a gift of forty pistoles. It was a lot of money for D'artagnan, and he sought advice from the Three Musketeers on how to spend it.

As per Aramis' suggestion, a house was taken on rent for D'artagnant to live in. Porthos suggested that D'artagnan get himself a lackey to help with the household chores. In addition, as per Athos' request, D'artagnan took all his friends to a delicious dinner.

D'artagnan soon settled into his new life of a Cadet in the King's Army. He continued training and honing his combat skills, and would spend most of his spare time with the Three Musketeers. D'artagnan got to know very little about the lives of his friends, though. Athos revealed that he was a nobleman who had suffered through a rather terrible love affair in the past, Porthos confessed

that he was greatly in love with a duchess whom he was going to marry soon, and Aramis said that he was determined to become a priest once he quit the job of a Musketeer.

Life was going along rather well for young D'artagnan, but gradually, he had to come face to face with the fact that the money he had been rewarded by the King was coming to an end. One day, D'artagnan was sitting in his house, lost in deep worry, when his attendant, Planchet, announced the arrival of a man named Monsieur Bonacieux.

"Alright, let him in at once," said D'artagnan. "I think I have heard this name somewhere before."

A man, perhaps in his early fifties, walked into the room. He seemed rather concerned about something, yet was trying hard to maintain a smile on his lips.

"Good evening, Sir!" D'artagnan greeted the gentleman at once. "How can I be of assistance to you?"

Monsieur Bonacieux sighed heavily and began, "Noble Sir, I have heard of your fame as a cadet, and

I also see you spend your time with those valiant Three Musketeers. Therefore, when I fell into this great deal of trouble, I felt that you alone would perhaps be able to understand my predicament."

D'artagnan was intrigued by the old man. "Do go on, Monsieur Bonacieux," urged D'artagnan.

Monsieur Bonacieux had turned extremely pale as D'artagnan asked him to continue and, after a short pause, he said, "Well Sir, to put it rather bluntly, my wife has been kidnapped!" And the old man started to sob.

D'artagnan was rather shocked on listening to the old man. "What? Where? How did it happen?"

Monsieur Bonacieux tried to control his emotions and replied, "You see Sir, she is one of the ladies-in-waiting for the Queen. She knows quite a lot about the Queen's private affairs and, therefore, when she was leaving the palace for our home yesterday, a tall man with a black patch over his eyes jumped out of a carriage took her away!"

D'artagnan's eyes grew wide on hearing about the abductor and he excitedly asked, "You say the

man had a black patch over his eye? Did he also have a scar on one of his cheeks?"

Monsieur Bonacieux tried to recollect more about the kidnapper and then agreed. "Yes Sir, I remember quite distinctly. He did have an eye-patch over his right eye and a scar on his face."

"The nobleman from Meung. It is indeed strange as to how our paths keep crossing," D'artagnan muttered to himself. Turning to the old man, the young cadet asked, "And do you think you can help me further? Do you know what is the exact reason for them to take your wife away so violently?"

Monsieur Bonacieux shrugged his shoulders casually and said, "But of course, it must surely have something to do with the Queen's torrid love affair!"

D'artagnan stiffened on hearing these words and very softly, he asked, "Queen Anne's love affair? Are you certain about what you are saying? This is sheer treason and I will not bear any part in it!"

Monsieur Bonacieux smiled and replied, "But Sir, you are perhaps the only person in the whole of Paris not to know about it. It is common knowledge that the marriage between King Louis XIII and Queen Anne was just a political ploy to secure peace between France and Spain. Everyone knows that she has actually given her heart away to the Duke of Buckingham, the Prime Minister of England."

D'artagnan continued to stare agape at his guest. "How is it that you know so much about the Queen's private life?" D'artagnan asked, his tone rather stern.

"My wife, Constance, she tells me everything. I can also tell you that the Queen is rather scared about the recent political developments...she thinks it is a ploy by Cardinal Richelieu to disgrace her and something is surely afoot," revealed Monsieur Bonacieux.

D'artagnan narrowed his gaze on the man seated before him once again, and asked, "You have given me quite a lot of information. I just hope that all this is true!"

"By all means it is, Sir. Why would I lie to you and also expect you to find my wife? I swear on

my name, Bonacieux, that I have told you only the truth!" declared the old man.

"Why is it that your name sounds to familiar to me?" D'artagnan asked, unable to hide his curiosity.

Monsieur Bonacieux smiled, even though his face still looked rather scared, and replied, "Perhaps my name rings a bell in your mind because I am your landlord, Monsieur. I was hoping that instead of paying me my due rent for the past three months, you would rather help rescue my wife."

D'artagnan realised that his shrewd landlord had put him in a corner and he would now definitely have to help the man find his wife again. "Alright, Monsieur Bonacieux, I shall take up your case at once. Have you received any message from the kidnappers?"

Bonacieux's face lit up at once and he started fishing into his pockets. "Ah, I had almost forgotten about this." He soon took out a piece of paper and handed it to D'artagnan. The young cadet glanced over it at once and read, "Your wife is safe. She will come back to you when we decide so. Till then you are to maintain silence. Try finding her and you will go to prison."

D'artagnan was puzzled on reading the message. Could Monsieur Bonacieux be right? Could Cardinal Richelieu be involved in some kind of a plot to oust the King?

"I shall definitely look into the case. You please go home and take rest," D'artagnan advised a much more relieved Monsieur Bonacieux.

As the landlord left, D'artagnan instructed Planchet to go and find the Three Musketeers and ask them to rush over at once. Soon, Athos, Parthos and Aramis were sitting before D'artagnan, and he recounted to his friends all that Monsieur Bonacieux had told him.

Suddenly, as D'artagnan was debating with the Three Musketeers as to what their next move should be, Monsieur Bonacieux stumbled into the room, screaming, "They have got me, they are after me! I will land up at Bastille, I just know it!" Four of the Cardinal's Guards rushed in behind the landlord, trying to apprehend the old man.

Porthos tried to move forward and stop them, but D'artgnan held him back and exclaimed, "Gentlemen! We all serve the King and the Cardinal, we won't stop you from carrying out your duties. Please take this man away!"

Monsieur Bonacieux stared at D'artagnan in disbelief. "But I trusted you, you told me that you would save me," he muttered in shock.

D'artagnan quickly whispered to the landlord, "And I intend to do just that. But for that I need to be free outside, and not in prison with you. Calm down and go with them quietly!"

Monsieur Bonacieux saw reason in D'artagnan's words and he peacefully surrendered before the Cardinal's Guards at once. Athos gave a quick glance towards D'artagnan, gesturing to the young cadet that he had indeed done the right thing.

Chapter Five

Finding Constance

D'artagnan had already started work in collecting evidence about Madame Bonacieux's kidnapping by the nobleman from Meung. Since the Cardinal's Guards were keeping strict watch on Bonacieux's house, D'artagnan had to find another way to observe the goings-on in the apartment. He soon found a vantage point for himself, on the second floor of the house. He kept constant vigil, along with Planchet, through a hole in one of the wooden floors there.

Many days had passed, when D'artagnan one day heard the desperate cries of a woman in distress. "Please let me pass," the woman kept telling the Guards, "I am Constance Bonacieux and I live here."

D'artagnan's expression changed colour at once. "It is her, Planchet, she has come back home."

But it seemed the Guards were in no mood to listen to her, even as she tried to explain to them that she lived in that house with her husband. D'artagnan turned to Planchet and said, "I think they are trying to tie her up and then take her away. I can't let that happen, my friend!"

So saying, D'artagnan climbed out through the open window and gently lowered himself into the apartment below. He could now hear the voices coming from the room before him. Without wasting another moment, D'artagnan took his sword in his hand and leapt into the room, breaking the door behind him. The sounds of steel clashing against each other filled the air for the next few moments, till four of the Cardinal's Guards ran out of there, bleeding profusely.

D'artagnan then turned his attention to the young woman sitting on a chair in the room, trying to come to grips with all that was happening before her. D'artagnan estimated that she must have been around twenty-five at the most and muttered to himself, "This is why I can never understand arranged marriages... her husband is clearly much too old for her."

The lady was stirring slightly, and seeing D'artagnan standing before her, she softly asked, "I must thank you for saving me from those horrible guards, Monsieur... but who are you and what are you doing here?"

D'artagnan was indeed quite smitten by young Constance Bonacieux. With a small courtsey, the young cadet humbly submitted, "I was hired by your husband to help in your rescue. However, I see you have managed that task quite by yourself."

Constance smiled and replied, "Well, they had me locked up in this room. But I managed to slip out through the window, using several sheets as a rope!"

D'artagnan was rather impressed by the lady's sharp attitude and remarked, "You are indeed quite intelligent, Madame! However, I must warn you to leave this place with me at once. The Cardinal's

Guards do not like to face defeat and will surely be back with much greater force."

Constance seemed to be greatly troubled at that thought. She got up from the chair and said, "Monsieur, I need your help to get to the palace tonight itself!"

D'artagnan listened in shock as Constance started to get ready to make the journey to the palace at such a late hour. "You do realise the risk that you take?" asked the young man. "After all, you were abducted right from outside the Queen's quarters. Don't you think we should first try and get you to a safe location?"

But Constance was adamant. "No, it is absolutely essential that I go there, or Queen Anne will be in great trouble. Oh please, Monsieur, my husband would never do this for me, but I know you will."

D'artagnan was quite smitten by Constance. He felt something about her that he had never felt for any lady before. Knowing fully well the risk that lay before him, he agreed to escort her to the palace.

They walked along for quite some time till they reached a rather large building. Constance asked D'artagnan to wait for her in the shadows, and went up to the mammoth door of the house. She knocked on it thrice and the door swung open. D'artagnan watched as a man came out and, keeping his hand on Constance's shoulders walked with her in the direction of the palace.

D'artagnan was filled with unbearably jealous rage. Constance, it seemed to him, had just offered him her heart and here she was, walking with another man! Without another moment to waste, D'artagnan rushed out from where he was hiding and pulled the man with Constance around.

"Draw, if you dare!" he challenged the stranger, who, too, drew his sword out in a flash. Constance immediately came in between the two men and pushed them away. "Milord please!" she begged the unknown man, and turning to D'artagnan, she exclaimed, "I asked you to follow us, Monsieur, not to get us into further trouble."

But D'artagnan was not listening to her any more. Dumbfounded, he stared at the stranger and the words slipped out of his lips, "Milord?" He at once fell to his knees and respectfuly asked, "Why, you are the Duke of Buckingham! I am so sorry, Milord, my love for Madame Bonacieux got the better of me."

The Duke of Buckingham put his sword back in his sheath at once and replied with a gentle laugh, "You are indeed a brave man to protect your woman this way! What is your name, Monsieur?"

"D'artagnan, Milord! I am a cadet in the King's Army. May I be of any more assistance to you tonight?" D'artagnan asked.

The Duke of Buckingham nodded his head and said, "But of course! You must follow us to the palace and make sure that no one gets in our way."

D'artagnan immediately slipped back and the Duke of Buckingham continued his journey with Constance to the palace. The young Gascon kept watch as the two of them walked passed two heavy iron doors and made their way into the palace.

Constance led the Duke through a dimly lit staircase into a room. As soon as the Duke entered, he fell to his knees and softly whispered, "Anne, I have arrived, my love!"

Queen Anne who had already been waiting there for the English Prime Minister, nervously replied, "Milord, you should not have come here. You know how tense the entire political scene is. Cardinal Richelieu is constantly trying to find some way to catch us red handed…"

"But Anne," interrupted the Duke of Buckingham, "I just had to see you. Nothing seemed to be important anymore. I just had to meet you, spend time with you."

Queen Anne gave a tired smile and explained, "But Milord, I do not want to embarrass the King, whatever may be the truth between us. We might find some better way of being together."

The Duke seemed to understand her concerns and replied, "Then I shall leave for England at once. But you must give me something that you hold dear to you, something that I can wear myself, to remember you while we stay apart. Anything at all will do!"

The Queen was at that time wearing a ribbon studded with twelve large diamonds. Not wanting the Duke to stay at the palace any longer and bring misfortune on himself, Queen Anne took off the ribbon and handed it over to the Duke. "Here, take this and go at once," she pleaded with her beloved.

The Duke of Buckingham stared into the Queen's eyes and promised, "We shall meet again, Anne... but not like this, in the dark, alone. We shall meet now when I have conquered France and you and I will live together for the rest of our lives," and so saying, the Duke walked out of the room.

Constance and D'artagnan escorted the British Prime Minister to the large house where he was staying incognito and he was helped into a coach which would take him straight to the harbour and from there, to England.

Chapter Six

Spying

The Cardinal's Guards were busy dragging a terrified Monsieur Bonacieux into the Bastille, the most well-guarded prison in the whole of France, where political prisoners were left to rot for the rest of their lives. Monsieur Bonacieux was taken through a maze of corridors to a chamber that had been built underground. An officer of the Cardinal's Guards was already seated there, writing something in a log book.

"Hmm! So you are Bonacieux. Well, my good man, seems like you and your wife are going to spend a long time in Bastille," the officer barked.

Monsieur Bonacieux was shivering and replied respectfully, "But my lord, what have I done? I am innocent!"

"You and your wife have been found plotting against King Louis XIII of France! You will be severely punished for this," the officer threatened.

Bonacieux's expression changed to one of fear and surprise as he pleaded, "Why, that is impossible my lord! I have never in my whole life done anything against the King. And my wife is one of the Queen's most favourite ladies-in-waiting and, moreover, my wife has already been kidnapped!"

The officer was a little surprised to hear this and he asked, "Kidnapped? And can you identify the man who abducted Madame Bonacieux?"

"Of course I can!" replied Monsieur Bonaieux, feeling that the officer was finally realising his mistake. "He was a tall man, looked quite like a nobleman, and he did have a black patch over his right eye and there was also a scar on his face."

The officer had been making hurried notes in his log book till then, but on hearing Bonacieux's description of the kidnapper, he stopped immediately and kept staring at Bonacieux's face. After a few moments had elapsed, the officer called one of the guards who had brought Monsieur Bonacieux in and whispered, "I think it is best if the Cardinal himself interrogates the prisoner!"

Even before Bonacieux could understand what was going to happen to him, he was quickly dragged away by four of the Cardinal's Guards and pushed into a sealed carriage. Monsieur Bonacieux was too scared to ask any questions, as the carriage spead along the cobbled streets of Paris.

The carriage finally stopped before a large mansion and Monsieur Bonacieux was taken in through its huge back doors. As they entered a large hall, Monsieur Bonacieux saw a man standing before him. He was of average height, with a small red cap on his head. He was wearing elegant red robes which swept the floor as he walked. It was his gaze that terrified Monsieur Bonacieux the most. Why would it not, Cardinal Richelieu, the most powerful man in the whole of France, was staring straight at him.

In a rather still, but cold voice, Cardinal Richelieu spoke to Bonacieux, "You speak even after committing treason, Monsieur Bonacieux?"

The poor old man slumped to his feet in fright. Crying out of fear, Monsieur Bonacieux muttered, "Monseigneur, I am but a loyal servant of His Majesty, why would I do anything to destabalise his rule? Quite the contrary, Sir, I myself am a victim. My wife has been abducted, and when I told the same thing to your officer back in the Bastille, he sent me here to you at once."

The Cardinal turned away at once, slightly unnerved on hearing Monsieur Bonacieux's words. "Has she now? And have you been able to see the man who did this evil deed?"

Monsieur Bonacieux went on the describe the nobleman with the black patch once again, as the Cardinal looked on, seeming quite amused at what had happened. "Look clearly then," directed the Cardinal and said, "Is this the man who kidnapped your wife?"

So saying, the Cardinal clapped his hands and a man came into the hall from behind the curtain. "It is him! it is him!" screamed Bonacieux, as the nobleman with the black patch walked into the room.

The Cardinal seemed to be quite amused at Bonacieux's reaction and calling his guards, he said, "Take Monsieur Bonacieux away from here. I may need to speak to him in a while."

As soon as they were alone, the Cardinal turned to the nobleman and said, "Rochefort, my dear friend, your standard of work has been slipping. These days even fools like Bonacieux are able to identify you. What happened, where is your focus these days?"

Rochefort looked unhappy for having let down the Cardinal and bowing his head in shame, he replied, "Forgive me for this, My Lord, ashamed as I am to admit it, but your most humble spy has made yet another mistake. Constance, Bonacieux's wife has escaped. However, I don't feel it will cause us any harm."

The Cardinal turned to Rochefort and looked at him enquiringly. "I do bring some other rather exciting news my lord, something that you will benefit much more from."

"Well then, let me hear it," said the Cardinal. Rochefort began, "It is like this Monseigneur, the

Duke of Buckingham is presently on his way back to England after having a rather secret rendevous with Queen Anne at the palace."

A malicious smile quickly spread across the Cardinal's lips and he quipped, "Go on, tell me more about this meeting between lovers!"

"One of the Queen's ladies-in-waiting told me that the Queen apparently gave the Duke a ribbon with some twelve diamonds on it, as a token of her love. Only that the ribbon was actually a gift from the King on the Queen's last birthday!" Rochefort added.

"Ah!" cried the Cardinal, extremely happy at these recent developments. "I shall instruct Milady to look into the matter. She is at Court everyday and she will get me two of the diamonds on that ribbon. The Queen will pay the price for such treachery!"

The Cardinal quickly sat down at the table and started scribbling something hurriedly on a piece of paper. Sealing the contents, he handed it over to Rochefort and said, "Give this to your fastest messenger and tell him to take it to London at once.

Milady will know what to do. And oh, Rochefort, on your way out please ask the guards to bring that bumbling fool back in."

Monsieur Bonacieux was howling as he was brought back to the Cardinal. "Oh spare me, Monseigneur! I have done no harm to the crown or to my country. Please let me go!"

The Cardinal placed his arms around Bonacieux's shoulders, helped him stand up and said, "Oh come now, my friend! Did I even for once doubt your loyalty to me?"

Monsieur Bonacieux was quite surprised to hear the Cardinal talk that way. In all his excitement, he turned to one of the guards and asked, "Did the most powerful man in France just call me his friend?"

Cardinal Richelieu smiled on hearing Monsieur Bonacieux's words and, embracing the old landlord, said, "My apologies, my friend, for treating you so shabbily! Here, take this as a token of my gratitude for all that you have done, and all that you will do for me in the future surely!" So saying, the

Cardinal handed over a bag of a hundred pistoles to Monsieur Bonacieux.

"Oh heavens be praised! I shall forever remain your indebted servant, Monsiegneur! You are indeed too kind!" cried an elated Bonacieux.

As the old landlord was escorted out of the mansion, Cardinal Richelieu thought to himself, "And now I have someone to spy on the clever Madame Bonacieux!"

Chapter Seven

The Cardinal's Plans

It was almost two weeks after Cardinal Richelieu sent Milady his letter about stealing two of the diamond studs in the ribbon that the Queen had given the Duke of Buckingham, that Milady's letter reached the Cardinal. "I have secured the diamonds, but need money to come back to Paris."

The Cardinal rubbed his hands in glee and decided, "Hmm! It will take around five days for me to send Milady her money and then she will take another five days to return to Paris. That gives me around ten days to accomplish my plot."

Without wasting any time at all, Cardinal Richelieu rushed off to meet the King. As he was escorted into the King's chambers, he began with

his scheme to humiliate the King and the Queen. "Your Majesty, if you do not mind my saying it, doesn't our beloved Queen look rather displeased these days?"

King Louis XIII seemed quite unaware about his wife's displeasure and he at once asked the Cardinal what he could do to make her feel better.

"I would suggest that we have a grand ball. The Queen can then wear that fabulous collar that you had gifted her, you know, the one with the diamonds, and I am sure she will feel like her old self once again," the Cardinal assured the King.

The King was quite eager to organise a ball, for that would give him, too, a break from the political tensions that he had been trying to sort out for a while. "When do you think we should hold the ball?" he asked the Cardinal.

"Considering the arrangements that have to be done, I should suggest that we plan it for the third of October. Ten days should be more than enough to get everything ready!" the Cardinal declared.

As the King started to go to the Queen's chambers, the Cardinal called out once again from behind, "Do remember to tell her about the ribbon!"

The unsuspecting King Louis XIII told his wife, the beautiful Queen Anne, about the ball and even asked her to wear the diamond studded ribbon for the festivities. The poor Queen tried to hide her shock as soon as she heard the King speak about the diamonds. By the time the King left, Queen Anne was trembling. She was completely at a loss as to what was to be done and had not the slightest idea of the Cardinal's role in bringing about her present predicament.

Suddenly, amidst the Queen's dilemma, a voice called out to her from behind the curtain. "My lady, I think I can be of some assistance in this matter!"

As she saw Constance come towards her, the poor Queen tried to force a smile on her scared face and asked, "Can you, my dear Constance? Do you know a way in which we can get those diamonds back?"

"Why yes, my lady! I can find a messenger whom we can trust and he can get the diamond studded ribbon back for you before the ball. But I will need a letter in your own hand for the Duke," Constance assured her.

Queen Anne at once got busy in writing the letter and as she handed it over to Constance, she also gave her a bag containing a thousand pistoles, adding, "Your messenger will need this to go and come back from England as fast as he can."

Constance ran home at once and found her husband waiting for her. "My dear, it is so lovely to see you after such a long time. But right now, I have some work which can earn you quite some money!"

"Money?" exclaimed the greedy Bonacieux.

"Yes! All you need to do is take this letter to London and come back with a package for the Queen!" explained Constance.

But the colour faded from Bonacieux's face as he heard his wife speak. "Bah! All you can think of are conspiracies. And that too against someone as fine as the Cardinal! Cardinal Richelieu has told me all about them."

A look of fear came over Constance at once. "The Cardinal?" she asked, trying to figure out if she had heard him correctly, "Did you say that you have heard of these plots from the Cardinal?"

"Why yes! I am a friend of the Cardinal's and I tell you, he takes very good care of me. Here," he said, raising the bag of a hundred pistoles that had been given to him by the Cardinal, "look at what he has given me." As he put the bag down, Bonacieux added, "There is no way that I am going to do anything against the Cardinal for that wretched Queen of yours."

Constance shuddered. She realised that had she said anything more to her husband, the Cardinal would get to know all about their plans. Not to mention that the Queen would be disgraced at the ball for sure.

But watching her expression change so rapidly, even a fool like Bonacieux knew that he had made a mistake. He knew he should have learnt about the entire plan and then gone over to the Cardinal and told him about it.

Monsieur Bonacieux tried to cajole his wife into telling him more. "Now, now, my dear! I may have been a little too hasty with my sharp words. What is it that you want me to do for your Queen?"

Constance had by now understood her husband's true motives and replied with a smile, "Oh, it's nothing important. The Queen just needed a few items to be purchased from London, that's all!"

Monsieur Bonacieux knew that his wife was now aware of his intentions, but the Cardinal would be happy with even half the information. Therefore, he left for the Cardinal's mansion at once.

No sooner was he out of the door then Constance screamed after him, "You moron! Now you are working as a spy for the Cardinal? There was never any love between us, but whatever there was has now turned to hate! I'll see to it that you pay for this treachery!"

But even as Constance screamed at her husband in absentia, she was still concerned about how to get the message across to the Duke of Buckingham and save the Queen's honour. As she sat down

on a chair, a voice called out from above, "Er... Constance, if you don't mind opening the door, perhaps I can solve your troubles!"

Chapter Eight

For the Queen!

As Constance opened the door, she saw D'artagnan standing there before her, smiling from ear to ear. Constance blushed and said, "So you heard everything that was said here?"

D'artagnan shrugged and replied, "I heard a little bit... like the Queen needs someone to go to London and bring back something for her. If you don't mind, I think I can be of some help in the matter."

Before Constance could say anything more, D'artagnan added, "I think it is better that we go upstairs and discuss the rest of the matter there. Your husband could be back and I don't think we need to let him know about the Queen's plans!"

As soon as they were back upstairs, Constance embraced D'artagnan and said, "Thank you so much, my dear. I don't know what I would have done without you!"

She then handed him the letter that Queen Anne had written for the Duke of Buckingham and also gave him a bag of coins. "Here, take these hundred pistoles that my husband got. You'll need it for your travels to England."

D'artagnan smiled as he took the money from her and said, "So I am to use the Cardinal's money to save the Queen from the Cardinal. If you think about it, it's quite funny!"

But, even before they could laugh at the joke he made, D'artagnan suddenly pressed his fingers softly on Constance's lips and gestured to her to keep silent. "Did you hear that? I think someone is in your flat. I think it is your husband and he is not alone."

The two of them then rushed to the room with the hole in the floor and D'artagnan pressed his eye against it to see what was happening downstairs.

Constance too crept up close to him and tried to listen in on her husband's conversation.

"I don't know where she is. But knowing Constance, she must have gone back to the palace to speak to the Queen about her failure," Bonacieux told his friend.

D'artagnan pressed closer and tried to identify the man who had accompanied Bonacieux back to his house. "Why, it is the nobleman from Meung! The one with the patch over his eye..."

Constance immediately added, "But that is Count Rochefort. He is the one who abducted me from outside the palace. I do think that he works for the Cardinal."

Rochefort stared at Bonacieux and barked, "I have not seen a bigger fool than you! You should have taken that letter and then come to the Cardinal!"

Bonacieux replied casually, "Don't worry. That fool of a wife I have will surely never suspect me. As soon as she comes back, I shall coax her into giving me the letter!"

"And you are certain that she will not get suspicious?" asked Rochefort, slightly concerned.

Bonacieux laughed and replied, "You need to have brains to understand such matters and Constance has none!"

Constance was furious hearing her husband speak that way about her and softly muttered, "Oh! I could just kill that fat fool!"

Even as Rochefort and Bonacieux continued their conversation, Constance turned to D'artagnan and said, "We are getting late. Let these scoundrels keep talking, I should start off towards the palace and console the Queen. You, meanwhile, should be on your way to London at once!"

D'artagnan agreed and kissing Constance goodbye, he started towards Monsieur de Tréville's office. He would first have to take permission to leave his duty for a few days and also obtain a pass for him to travel to England.

Monsieur de Tréville heard out D'artagnan's story about the Cardinal's plot. At the end, he grimly commented, "This is not good at all. It could spell doom for the country. You do realise, though, that the Cardinal will try everything in his capacity to stop you from crossing the English Channel?"

"Yes Sir, I do undertand that he will want to make sure that his plans succeed. I would, therefore, like to ask for your permission to allow Athos, Porthos and Aramis come with me as well. That way, even if we face obstacles on the path, at least one of us is sure to reach England and save the Queen's honour."

Monsieur de Tréville was appreciative of the idea and at once had passes made for D'artagnan and the Three Musketeers.

In the next few hours, the four friends were riding their horses towards Calais, the port from where they could get the boat to Dover, England.

Everything was moving as planned until the next day when the four friends stopped at an inn to eat and drink something before resuming their journey. It was there that a drunk sitting on the opposite table turned to Porthos and declared, "I think we should all drink a toast to the Cardinal."

Loyal as he was, Porthos agreed to the man's proposal, but added, "I think that after that we should also all raise our glasses to the health of our King!"

The drunk was not pleased one bit on hearing that and, banging his fist on the table, he declared, "Never have I ever drunk in the name of that wretched King and neither will I let anyone else," and so saying, the man took out his sword and pointed it towards Porthos.

The Musketeer too dragged his sword out of its sheath and turning to his friends, he said, "I think you should carry on without me. I need to teach this man some manners when talking about the King!"

The three friends agreed and were soon on their way to Calais on their horses. They came across a tract of road which was being repaired by some workmen. The friends paid no attention and continued racing across, when suddenly, all the workmen dropped their instruments and, raising their muskets, started firing at the King's soldiers.

They had almost made it out of their range of fire, when a stray shell hit Aramis on the shoulder.

The brave Musketeer did not flinch and continued to ride with his friends. However, after a long time of travelling, Aramis declared that he could not continue due to severe blood loss and asked his friends to go to without him while he went looking for help to treat his wounds.

Athos and D'artagnan then continued on their journey alone. It was clear that these were the Cardinal's traps, but they kept riding, well aware that there were bound to be more on the way. Finally, after travelling for more than a day, they were both extremely tired and decided to take some rest at an inn.

As they entered the inn and asked for a room, the innkeeper looked at them carefully and insisted that he would require them to pay for their lodgings in advance. Athos felt it would be wiser to avoid an argument on the issue and followed the innkeeper into his office.

Just as he entered, four armed officers of the Cardinal's Guard sprung from within and grabbed Athos. The Musketeer was completely trapped in their iron grip and could not fight his way out. "Run, D'artagnan! You are now our last hope. I shall deal with these men, you head to Calais at once!"

D'artagnan, though sad that he could be of no assistance to his friend, understood the gravity of the situation. He leapt on his horse and rode away from the inn, deciding that it would be more prudent to ride on continuously rather than stop on the way and get into trouble. After a long journey, he finally arrived at Calais.

As he walked towards the harbour from where the ships for England were to leave, he saw the shadow of a tall man approach the Captain of the ship. D'artagnan strained his ears and heard the man say, "I need to travel to England."

The Captain of the ship replied, "As per the Cardinal's orders, only those with a pass from His Eminence can board the ship."

The man put his hand into his coat and taking out a slip of paper, handed it over to the Captain. He looked at it and replied, "Sure, Sir, you are most welcome on my humble steamer. But we still have an hour before we leave. Maybe you would prefer spending some time at the inn down the road!"

As the man turned to walk towards the inn, D'artagnan gasped. "Count Rochefort! Finally, our paths cross again!"

Without wasting a moment, D'artagnan jumped from where he was hiding and came before Rochefort. "Quickly now," he ordered, pointing his sword towards the nobleman, "hand over that pass and I shall consider ourselves even!"

But instead of obliging, Count Rochefort swiftly took his sword out and replied, "I see you do not have your friends with you for protection!"

D'artagnan smiled and replied, "I am more than enough for you! Now hand over that pass peacefully, or I have no qualms in taking it from your dead body!"

Rochefort did not bother replying anymore and the two started fighting each other. D'artagnan fought bravely, but Rochefort, too, knew how to wield his weapon with great skill. Finally, however,

D'artagnan was able to wound the spy thrice, each time crying, "One for Athos!", "One for Porthos!" and "One for Aramis!"

Considering Count Rochefort dead, D'artagnan slipped his hand into the Count's coat to extract the pass. But the Count was merely wounded and he quickly grabbed his sword and drove it through D'artagnan's chest, exclaiming, "And this one is for you!"

D'artagnan furiously stabbed Rochefort in the shoulder and said, "True! One for me!"

D'artagnan was able to retrieve the pass for his journey to England and was on board the steamer when it left for Dover. His wound was not very serious and he was able to apply a rough bandage to it to make the bleeding stop.

As D'artagnan stepped on English soil for the first time next morning, he knew that he would have to reach London, as soon as he could, to inform the Duke about the Cardinal's plot. While his horse was being saddled, D'artagnan looked around to see the passengers boarding a steamer for

Calais. He kept looking around when, suddenly, he thought he had seen one of the passengers before. She was a beautiful blonde woman and D'artagnan recognised her instantly as the lady Rochefort had spoken to in Meung. "I think he had called her Milady! I wonder what she is doing here? Is she a part of the Cardinal's conspiracy?"

But he knew that he would have to deal with Milady later. He had first to head to London and make his way to the Duke's mansion, where he arrived quite late in the evening.

The Duke's valet ushered D'artagnan indoors and asked, "And who am I to say is calling?"

D'artagnan smiled and replied, "The man who challenged him to a duel in Paris a few days ago!"

D'artagnan did not have to wait for too long as the Duke of Buckingham came rushing in. "What has happened to her? Is she alright?"

D'artagnan sighed deeply and replied, "She is for now... but she will be in great trouble if we do not hurry. She has written this letter for you!"

The Duke tore through the envelope and read through the contents of the letter quickly. "Oh my poor girl! This is terrible. Come, we do not have much time to lose!"

The Duke of Buckingham led D'artagnan through the staircase until they reached a locked room. The Duke took out a gold key which hung from his neck and opened the door. The two of them then walked into a candlelit chapel and reached the very end of it. A portrait of Queen Anne hung right above the altar, from where the Duke retrieved a small wooden box. He deftly ran his fingers through the small lock on the box and, as he opened it, took out the diamond studded ribbon that Queen Anne had given him.

But as the Duke was handing it over to D'artagnan, his face flushed with fear and he screamed, "Oh holy heavens!"

D'artagnan could not understand the Duke's alarm and asked, "Milord, is anything the matter?"

"The ribbon, the last two diamonds are missing! Look!" exclaimed the Duke of Buckingham as he pointed to the bottom end of the ribbon.

D'artagnan started twitching nervously, as he confirmed, "Are you sure of this, Milord?"

The Duke replied, wondering at the same time who could have stolen the last two diamonds, "Quite certain, look at how the ribbon has been cut here. But wait, yes, I am quite certain about this, it must have been Milady de Winter. She spent quite a lot of time with me the day I last wore this to court. She must have taken it to the Cardinal!"

D'artagnan too now shared the Duke's concern and informed him, "I saw her boarding the steamer for Calais when I reached here. Those diamonds are already on their way to the Cardinal."

The Duke started walking out of the chapel and gestured to D'artagnan to follow him. "We do not have any time to lose then," he informed the French cadet and led through an entire series of corridors, till they reached a room right at the rear of the mansion. The court jeweller had his workshop there and the Duke burst into the room.

"Here, take a good look at these," he told the head jeweller as he held out the ribbon and the diamonds in it for him. "How much do you think it will cost me to get two identical ones made?"

The jeweller carefully studied the remaining ten diamonds and replied, "I can make them for you for fifteen hundred pistoles each, Milord!"

The Duke dismissed the exorbitant price off with a shrug of his shoulders and said, "I don't care about the price, just tell me how long you will take to make them!"

The jeweller did some kind of mental math and replied respectfully, "They will be done in a week, Sire!"

D'artagnan jumped on hearing this and turning to the Duke, he said, "That will be too late, Milord! The Cardinal is organising the ball for the third of October. We will never be able to get these back to Paris in time!"

The Duke paused on hearing D'artagnan's information and then told the jeweller, "I will need these diamonds tomorrow morning. You can take any amount you want for them, but I want them tomorrow!"

"I shall see to it personally, Sire!" replied the jeweller and got to work immediately. True to his

word, he got the diamonds ready by morning. They were made so brilliantly that even the Duke could not say which one were the original and which ones were made over night.

Handing the ribbon over to D'artagnan, the Duke of Buckingham added, "I have arranged for a ship to take you back to France at once. A few horses and an escort will be available to take you to Paris as soon as you land in Calais. The rest is in your hands."

Just as D'artagnan was about to leave, the Duke added, "I shall never forget what you have done for your Queen, my good man. And even though we may soon fight each other in war as enemies, today we part as friends."

Chapter Nine

The Cardinal is Embarrassed

Thanks to the special arrangements made by the Duke of Buckingham, D'artagnan managed to reach Paris right on the eve of the ball. Before making his way to the palace, the young cadet first called on Monsieur de Tréville to ask about his friends. The Captain of the Musketeers assured him that they were all back in Paris and had all recovered from the wounds they had suffered on the journey to Calais.

D'artagnan then went straight to the palace, since his company was already stationed for duty there and he also had to pass on a package to the Queen.

Meanwhile, the ball was already underway and the King, along with Cardinal Richelieu, were awaiting the arrival of the Queen. A respectful

hush descended on the grand ball as the Queen of France made her way to the guests that had gathered there. But when he saw her neck bare, the King rushed to her at once and, in a displeased tone declared, "Madame, you have not worn the diamond studded ribbon I had asked you to. May I know the reason for your disobedience?"

The Queen looked at her husband, trying to muster all her courage and replied, "Sire, it was not my intention to go against your wishes, but seeing the crowd that has gathered here, I deemed it wise not to wear something so exquisite, lest it be taken from me!"

The King was not impressed with the Queen's justification and replied, "Well, Madame, all I can say is that I am extremely displeased with your actions."

The Queen tried to pacify the King by explaining, "Sire, it is not something that cannot be fixed. Please give me a little time and I shall return to my room and come back with the ribbon. Perhaps that will convince your Majesty!"

The King immediately agreed to Queen Anne's proposal and the Queen retreated into her chamber along with her ladies-in-waiting.

Just as the Queen walked away from there, the Cardinal placed a small box in the King's hands. The King looked at the Cardinal in surprise and the pontiff said, "Your Majesty, I insist that you take a look inside the box!"

The King opened it and his eyes grow wide open with surprise. There were two diamonds in the box, quite the same as were in the ribbon that the King had gifted the Queen sometime back. "What is the meaning of this?" the King said, rather furiously.

But the Cardinal merely smiled at the King and replied, "Your Majesty, in the event the Queen does indeed come back to the hall wearing the ribbon like you asked her to, which I seriously doubt, then I would ask you to count the number of diamonds in it."

The King was quite baffled at what he was hearing from the Cardinal, who was not done yet, "You will find that two diamonds will be missing from there… those two diamonds are here!" the Cardinal said, pointing at the box.

Before the King could ask any further questions, all eyes turned to the staircase. The Queen of France was coming to join her guests and around her neck was a spectacilar ribbon, adorned with exquisite diamonds.

The King was unable to control his smile, even as the Cardinal looked on, furious at his grand plan being ruined. As the Queen approached King Louis XIII, the King made a quick count of the number of diamonds in the ribbon. There were twelve of them!

"I hope your honour is satisfied," asked the Queen with a gentle courtesy.

The King was very pleased and replied, "Madame, you have filled my heart with joy. But I was of the opinion that you had lost two of your diamonds, ones which I would present to you today!" and the King handed her the box given to him by the Cardinal.

The Queen feigned surprise as she saw the two diamonds in the box and exclaimed, "Your Majesty, you are too kind! Now I shall have two more of these magnificent diamonds to add to this ribbon!"

The King passed an inquisitive look at the Cardinal, who tried to smile sheepishly and replied, "What can I do, Sire? I would not dare make a gift to her Highness of my own accord. I therefore, deemed it wise to give them to you for her!"

The Queen smiled at the Cardinal, rather sarcastically and expressed her gratitude. "Your Eminence is too kind! I can not find words to express my joy at this rather amazing gift!"

As the Cardinal bowed to the Queen's words, the lady walked away to join the rest of her guests. She made her way through the entire tide of people who had gathered there and came before a cadet in the King's Army who was on duty that evening.

She smiled at him appreciatively and put forward her hand to him, which he, falling to his knees, respectfully pressed to his lips. As the Queen walked away, she slipped a ring into the cadet's hand. D'artagnan was proud to have protected the honour of his Queen.

Only two people present there were witness to the Queen's affections towards this young cadet — the Cardinal Richelieu and a blonde lady who was accompanying the Cardinal, Milady de Winters. "Bah!" exclaimed the Cardinal, "That fool completely ruined my plans to humiliate the Queen and the King."

Milady whispered to the Cardinal, "And what are you going to do to him, Eminence? He deserves to be severely punished!"

"Punished?" asked the Cardinal with surprise. "If all my men were even half as good as that young man, there would hardly ever be any problem. No, quite the contrary, I would want him to work for me."

Milady was a little shocked on hearing the Cardinal speak that way and said, "Monseigneur, you might have other plans for this young fool, but I must have my revenge against him and that woman of his."

The Cardinal tried to place who Milady was talking of and declared, "Ah, the beautiful Madame

Bonacieux! Yes, she has become quite an obstacle in my path to humiliate the Queen. I will do something about her. Quick, ask Rochefort to come see me at once!"

Count Rochefort was still quite weak after his battle with D'artagnan. But when Milady told him about the Cardinal's plans to take revenge on Constance Bonacieux, he was quite pleased. Harming Constance would hurt D'artagnan — something he was looking quite forward to.

Chapter Ten

Love

D'artagnan was finally able to leave the ball in the early hours of the morning. He was on his way to meet Constance, the woman he was madly in love with. They had met once earlier that evening when he had arrived at the palace to give the Queen her diamond studded ribbon, and had agreed to meet later after the ball at his house.

He was almost home, when D'artagnan spotted the shadow of a carriage before him on the street. A brute seemed to be harassing the lady inside the carriage and she appered to be trying in vain to ward him off. Without wasting another moment, D'artagnan drew his sword, "Stop and say your prayers!" he cried as he ran towards the carriage.

Noticing D'artagnan approach, the hooligan ran into a dark alley. After unsuccessfully searching for him for a while, D'artagnan decided to head back to the carriage and check if the lady was alright.

As he looked in through the window, his face lit up and his heart started to beat very fast. Inside sat the most beautiful woman he had ever laid his eyes on. Her blonde hair strayed on to her face, she was trying to compose herself after such a terrible attack on her.

With great courage, D'artagnan asked the lady, "I hope that wicked creature has not managed to harm you?"

"You came just in time, Monsieur! I don't know what I would have done if a brave man like you had not been there to help," the lady muttered, still in some shock from the tragedy that had earlier befallen her.

D'artagnan blushed as he said, "It was my honour to save you, Madame!"

"Then I trust you will call on me tomorrow at my residence so I can express my gratitude to you

once again," pleaded the lady, as she handed him a card. "You will find my name and address in here," she added.

D'artagnan flipped the card over and stared in shock and horror as he learnt the name of the lady he had just saved. Milady de Winters.

Milady then wished D'artagnan a good night and her carriage soon sped across the street, leaving a stupefied D'artagnan wondering. Forgetting all his declarations of love to Constance, the poor man, was lost in deep thought."I don't know how I should react? I know I should be wary of this lady, but she fills my heart with a joy I cannot explain. I think I am in love!" exclaimed D'artagnan as he rushed back to his house.

D'artagnan waited at his house for Constance to arrive. But even though morning had already broken, there was no sign of her at all. Finally, seemingly outraged at Constance's breaking her promise and again, conveniently, oblivious to how easily he had been smitten with Milady, just a short while ago, D'artagnan decided to pay Athos a visit. After all, no one understood women better than Athos.

As he explained his predicament to the gentle Musketeer, Athos was not impressed at all. "Women should not be trusted, D'artagnan. I would advise you to stay clear of them, all of them," Athos declared angrily.

But D'artagnan was still depressed and did not want to believe what Athos was telling him. "But I thought Constance was different. Yet, here I am right now, and Constance is not with me. Did she only pretend to be in love with me so she would get her work done? You would know how it is, my friend. Surely, you have been in love before. What do you think?"

Athos cringed in disgust as D'artagnan said those last words and spat, "Me? In love? You must be out of your mind, D'artagnan. And to prove my point, allow me to tell you a story about one of my friends. He was a Count, a rich gentleman respected by everyone. And believe me when I tell you this, D'artagnan, that man could have married anyone he wished to."

Taking a swig from his glass, Athos continued, "But alas, the poor man went and fell in love with this sixteen year old girl. I admit, she was pretty, but he was not content with just keeping her as his mistress. No Sir, he married her, made her a part of his life, gave her his name, his family, everything."

D'artagnan watched as Athos' face changed colour completely. The Musketeer then added, "But it was not to last surely it could not last. They had gone riding that day. At one point during riding, the horse tripped and the two of them were thrown off. Even as my friend dusted himself off, his eyes searched for his beloved. The scene he saw, however, gave him the greatest shock of his life."

D'artagnan, who had been listening to the story with rapt attention, could not resist exclaiming, "Why? What had happened?"

Athos looked sullen as he explained, "When she slipped, her dress had dragged down leaving her shoulder bare and do you know what he saw on her bare arm? The fleur-de-lis! Yes, D'artagnan, it was that shameful mark branded on people who

steal the treasures of the church! It's the most horrible crime one can ever commit."

D'artagnan could feel Athos' pain as he was narrating the story. He seemed to be reliving the horror of the entire episode so deeply that it seemed it had happened to him and not the Count! It was truly the most scarring incident that could have perhaps ever happened in life. The young Gascon looked on at his friend, wanting to know what happened next. Athos continued, "Well, there was only one thing that my friend could do after that. He left her there, hanging from a tree. That is, after all, the law for those branded with the dastardly fleur de lis!"

Having said what he did Athos was silent for a few moments and D'artagnan, too, was shocked to hear the tale of the poor Count. Suddenly, unaware of his own words, Athos burst out, "And that, my dear friend, has never let me trust another woman again."

This last line made D'artagnan sit up. He earlier intuitive sense that Athos had been telling him his own tale had been confirmed.But he decided not to press on that doubt, particularly seeing the agony Athos was in. Instead, he clarified, "Then that lady is already dead, I presume?"

Athos nodded very slowly and replied, "I suppose so… I… I mean, my friend, the Count tried to hunt down her brother, a priest who lived in the same town, but there was no sign of him." Finishing his glass of wine, Athos finally ended his tale by saying, "That, then, was the end of it all!"

Athos looked very unhappy, as if he were reliving a moment that he had desperately tried to bury in his past once.

As evening approached and the consumption of a lot of wine made the two friends share more intimate thoughts, D'artagnan told Athos about his plans to pay a visit to Milady de Winters. Athos' drunken expression drained at once on hearing those words and he asked, "Didn't you tell me that this lady may well be working for the Cardinal?"

D'artagnan nodded his head sheepishly and replied, "I am certain that she is one of the

Cardinal's most important spies. But yes Athos, I cannot explain the feeling I get when I am before her. Those few minutes with her just made my head spin yesterday! I think I am quite in love with this lady."

An amused Athos listened to the wide-eyed young cadet and remarked, "And here you were, telling me about Constance's betrayal! Ha! Little did I think that you were going to betray Constance herself later in the evening. But all jokes aside, I must warn you to be careful my friend! You never know what this woman's ulterior motives may be."

Though he pretended to pay attention then, when the time came to meet Milady, D'artagnan brushed aside Athos' concerns and was soon on his way to meet the woman of his dreams. This one happy evening led to many more and soon, D'artagnan had visited Milady for more than a month.

On one such evening when D'artagnan called on Milady at her home, something rather unusual happened. Her maid, Kitty, let the young man inside and, without any warning, asked him quite directly, "Do I rightly believe Sir, that you are very much in love with my lady?"

D'artagnan was a little taken aback but, with a loving smile on his lips, replied, "That is correct, Kitty! I cannot explain how much it is that I love her. It is as if my heart belongs to her and her alone!"

Kitty seemed to be a little distressed on hearing this and replied, "Well then, Sir, I must tell you that Milady does not reciprocate your feelings one bit. You are just being used by this trecherous woman!"

D'artagnan's face turned red as he heard Kitty speak. "What?"

"I speak the truth, Monsieur! I have overheard her speak about you many a time and what she says is definitely not related to love," Kitty confessed.

D'artagnan did not know whether to believe her or not and asked, "And pray, of what use is it to you to tell me all this?"

"It is the same reason you call upon Milady every evening and I must do what I can to save you from any harm," was Kitty's rather brave response.

Before D'artagnan could quiz the maid any further, the sound of a door opening broke their conversation. "Quick, it is her... you must leave at once," exclaimed Kitty, as she started towards the door.

D'artagnan was just about to leave, when he decided that he should perhaps listen in on Milady's conversation and try to be certain of the maid's allegations. He hid inside the maid's closet and could hear Milady say something and then rush off into her bedroom. Very softly, the young cadet crept to the bedroom door and tried to listen to what Milady was saying.

"Has that young fool arrived yet?" was Milady's first question.

Kitty, who was helping Milady take off her hat, replied, "Not yet, my lady, which is rather strange if you ask me. Could it be that he has fallen in love with someone else?"

Milady started laughing and replied, "Come on now Kitty, you speak as if you don't know who I am! You know what happens to boys like

D'artagnan when I speak of love to them. Their legs give way and their hearts flutter. All the better for me to stomp on them after!"

Kitty pretended to be quite alarmed and immediately asked, "Then you do not love this boy?"

Milady stopped laughing at once and her tone turned very harsh after that. "Love? Him? I have nothing but hate for that scoundrel, that moron! He foiled my plans with that wretched Queen and that Duke of Buckingham. I will have my revenge, oh I will have my revenge yet!"

Milady paused momentarily, before she said again, "I have already taken care of that foolish woman he was in love with, that Bonacieux girl. And now it is his turn!"

It was only on hearing Constance's name that D'artagnan was beside himself with rage. The woman he thought he was in love with was perhaps the shrewdest witch he had ever seen in his entire life. Fearing the worst for Constance, D'artagnan rushed into the bedroom and seized Milady by her

neck. "What have you done to her? Speak right now or I shall silence you forever!"

Milady was completely taken by surprise and not knowing what to do, she reached for the knife she had on her and swung is desperately at D'artagnan. In the scuffle that ensued, Milady's brooch came off in D'artagnan's hand. Not wanting to physically hurt a woman, D'artagnan pulled himself up and took out his sword, pointing it at Milady.

The enraged spy of the Cardinal tried to dodge D'artagnan's pointed blade and, in the process, snagged her dress at her shoulder. As the piece of cloth fell, D'artagnan lost all control of his senses as he swaggered back. On Milady's shoulder was a small red mark. The fleur-de-lis.

D'artagnan was completely at a loss as to what he needed to do. Unable to command his senses once again, he merely ran out of the room and was on the streets. He could hear Milady scream after him, "You know my secret and for that you will now meet with your death! Beware you ignorant

fool, you will soon meet your maker. I will avenge this yet!"

D'artagnan continued to run right till he burst into Athos' room. "What happened? Why do you look so terrified?" cried Athos, trying to help D'artagnan stand straight.

"You will never believe what happened?" D'artagnan started, trying to control his wheezing breath. Athos looked at the cadet's hand and asked, "And this brooch has something to do with it?"

D'artagnan looked at his hand and found that he was still holding Milady's brooch. "Why yes," he said, "this belongs to her, to Milady!"

Athos took the brooch and looked at it carefully. The expression on his face turned to that of disgust and fear. "Then it is true, then it has to be true..."

D'artagnan looked surprised and asked, "What is true?"

"That she survived. Because there cannot be another of this... this brooch, this brooch belonged to my family for generations. And I remember clearly, she was wearing it that day, she was wearing it..."

D'artagnan was still lost and pressed further, "Who was wearing it, Athos? Please speak to me... tell me what happened?"

Athos, horrified at all that had happened, replied, "My wife. The Count I spoke of wasn't my friend, it was me. I am the Count de la Fere who became the Musketeer Athos because I could not bear her betrayal. The fleur-de-lis was on my wife, D'artagnan, she was the greatest sinner on this earth! And she still lives!"

Athos was in a state of complete shock. D'artagnan tried to support him, and helped him to a chair. Athos continued, "You need to hide from today onwards, D'artagnan. It is no longer safe for you, no place is safe for you... You know her identity, you know her secret. She will not spare you any longer, she will do everything she can to kill you."

D'artagnan tried to reassure his friend, "Do not worry so, my brave friend! I shall anyway be at La Rochelle from tomorrow with the rest of my company. The Huguenots have engaged us in battle and I think I will be safe there, far away from Paris."

Athos shook his head sadly, and said, "Like I said, no place is safe for you anymore. No, D'artagnan, we need to end this once and for all. Beware at all times and I will see what I can do about Milady!"

Chapter Eleven

For the Good of France

The population of France comprised majorly of two groups. Those who believed in Catholic Christianity and those who owed their religious allegiance to Protestantism, also known as the Huguenots. For many years, people of both faiths lived in peace, with the Protestants ruling over their own areas with no interference in their matters from the Catholic King, Louis XIII.

However, Cardinal Richelieu had other plans. He wanted France to come under the unified command of the King and, therefore, he waged a war against the Protestant ruled areas of the country. He had been successful mostly everywhere, except in the Huguenot town of La Rochelle. The battle there had

now lasted for a little over a year, with there being no major breakthrough for the King's army. Finally, the Cardinal's Guards and the King's Musketeers were also attached to the King's Army.

One day, therefore, when the siege of La Rochelle was still on, the Three Musketeers were off duty and decided to spend some time at the Red Dove Inn, a small tavern located a little out of the town. D'artagnan and his company were engaged in the actual battle at the time and therefore, he could not join the Musketeers.

Having made merry over a few bottles of wine, the Three Musketeers were soon on their way back to the battle front. Having travelled a few miles, they saw two horsemen approaching them. Sensing that there might be a large number of enemy soldiers in the vicinity, the Musketeers at once got ready to face an attack.

But the two horses slowed down as they reached them. The riders had their faces covered with their cloaks and could not be identified. But one of them turned to the Three Musketeers and said,

"Ah! Monsieurs Athos, Porthos and Aramis. It has indeed been my good fortune to run into you brave soldiers. Will you please accompany us to the Red Dove Inn immediately?"

Athos was a little surprised at the way in which the rider had recognised all three of them and was also ordering them to follow him. "Who are you? Identify yourself first, or feel the wrath of my sword!" Athos declared, placing his hand on the handle of his sword. Porthos and Aramis too followed his lead.

The rider then slowly unwrapped his cloak and stared coldly at the Three Musketeers, who could only gasp in surprise. "Why, your Eminence! Please forgive my impudence," pleaded Athos, bowing before Cardinal Richelieu.

"You were wise in questioning my identity, Monsieur Athos!" commended the Cardinal. "Now, if you will please escort us to the Red Dove Inn..." added the royal pontiff.

"We shall be honoured to guard you, Monseigneur," assured Athos, as the three friends turned their horses around in the direction of the Inn they had just come back from.

As soon as they reached the Inn, the Cardinal rushed in and asked the innkeeper, "Do you have some place here where these gentlemen can take some rest while I conclude my business?"

Bowing before the Cardinal, the innkeeper led the Musketeers to a room beside his office, and the Cardinal rushed off to one of the rooms on the first floor almost as if he was quite frequent in his visits to the inn.

A large stove pipe in the room where the Musketeers seated themselves helped keep them warm. Porthos and Aramis buried themselves playing odd games to spend their time, but Athos was slightly unnerved about the Cardinal's visit. As he paced around the room trying to identify the reason for the Cardinal's arrival at the Red Dove Inn, he thought he could hear some faint murmurs.

Athos pressed his ears close to the stove pipe and realised that they were coming down from the room above theirs. He could make out one of those voices as the Cardinal's and the other one as that of a lady. Motioning to Porthos and Aramis to be quiet, he tried to listen in on the conversation.

"I need you to go back to England right away," said the Cardinal.

The lady replied at once, "But Buckingham surely knows that it was me who stole the diamonds the last time. Why will he trust me again?"

"To hell with his trust! I need you to make sure that he remains in England. With this war we are fighting, the last thing we need is for the English to wage war against us. We cannot let that happen, you will not let that happen, Milady! Do what you must, but make sure that the Duke of Buckingham does not leave London!" barked the Cardinal, visibly upset.

Realising that the lady the Cardinal was speaking to was no other than Milady de Winters, Athos' ears were now fully alert. He wanted to catch every word that was exchanged between them after that.

"At least tell me what I should say to him!" Milady wanted to know.

"Simple! In the event that he sends his forces across the English Channel to fight the French armies, or even to help the Huguenots, the Queen will be in trouble. That should make him stop. Tell him that I have proof about the two of them and their various rendezvous!" replied the Cardinal.

Milady quickly interjected, "And if he still wants to attack us? Remember, with the King dethroned, it won't matter what proof we have about their affair!"

The Cardinal thought for a few moments, but unable to think of a solution, blurted out, "Just do whatever is necessary. But make sure that the Duke of Buckingham does not send his troops to assist the Huguenots, nor does he lead an expedition against France itself!"

It was clear to Athos that the Cardinal and Milady were hatching a conspiracy once again and he had to do something about it as soon as he had heard this entire conversation. He then heard Milady, "Your work shall be done, Your Eminence! But remember, once I come back to France I must be allowed to have my own little revenges!"

The Cardinal had obviously lost interest in the conversation, but feigned it, asking, "You mean against that Bonacieux woman? I thought she was in some prison... at Nantes I presume!"

"She was... but then the Queen found out about her and took her away to some convent. I don't know which one yet. Apparently, the Queen will not trust anyone with this information," Milady revealed.

The Cardinal replied at once, "That is hardly a big issue to resolve... I'll have the name of the convent for you by the time you come back from England."

"And about the other boy? The one who has made my life miserable recently. Why, even Rochefort would like to see something happen to him!" Milady declared.

"D'artagnan? Forget about him. Let this war in La Rochelle come to an end, and that young fool will be locked away somewhere in Bastille. And that will be the very end of him. Just focus on your work and bring me some good news this time," the Cardinal roared.

Milady was quite pleased at the proposal, and further suggested, "Sire, may I then ask you to write me a warrant... that way, if I am ever caught in France, I will not have to face any major problem with the law!"

Athos could hear nothing more. He was certain that the Cardinal had made himself busy writing the warrant that Milady desired. He knew that in all probability the Cardinal would leave for La Rochelle soon and Milady would start off on her way to England. He had to act, because lives were dependent on how efficiently he could plan things.

Turning to Porthos and Aramis, he told them, "When the Cardinal comes down, you two shall escort him to the battlefront."

"And what should we do if he asks for you?" Porthos asked at once. Athos replied, "Tell him that I have gone on ahead to see if the road is safe for travel. And listen, D'artagnan's life is in great danger. As soon as you get back, be by his side and make sure that nothing happens to him."

Athos then ran out and climbing his horse, he started off at once for La Rochelle. But instead of checking the road for trouble, he led his horse behind a huge tree and hid there, keeping watch to check whether the Cardinal and his friends were on their way.

As soon as he could spot their frames riding away at a distance, he turned back and made his way to the Red Dove Inn. He looked at the confused innkeeper and asked rather officially, "Is the woman still up there? The Cardinal wants me to give her a message!"

The innkeeper pointed towards the room and Athos rushed in. As the door opened, Milady turned around and started by saying, "How dare you..." and then she froze. Her face was covered with fear, she started sweating profusely — quite like she had seen a ghost.

"How... how... how... can it...be?" Milady gasped, unable to understand what she was seeing before her.

Athos smiled at her sadly and replied, "Yes, Milady, it is I. Just like you did not die that day, neither did the Count de la Fere. And just like you became Milady de Winters from Charlotte de

Beuil, similarly the Count de la Fere, too, became the humble Musketeer, Athos. And both of have lived, my dear, perhaps to see another day!"

Milady was still too dumbstruck to speak, as Athos continued, "Now I don't want to create trouble, but your dead body will lie here if you do not hand over the warrant that the Cardinal has written for you."

Milady was rooted to her spot. She could neither say or do anything. Athos saw a roll of paper in her hands and he snatched it away from her. He unfolded it and read its contents. "The bearer of this letter works under my command and whatever he or she may have done is for the good of France, so let him or her continue in their duties. December, 1627. Cardinal Richelieu."

Athos turned to Milady and said, "Rather impressive piece of paper you have here... But you are just going to be left with the fleur-de-lis, something that you can never get rid off!"

Milady was now regaining her composure and she hissed, "Hold your tongue, for I shall see to the end of this too..."

"I'll look forward to it. But for now listen to me carefully. I don't care what happens to the Duke of Buckingham, for he is still my enemy. But you harm one hair on D'artagnan's head and I shall make sure that this time you die for certain. Nothing should ever happen to him, or it is you I will seek out and watch bleed to death."

So saying, Athos charged out of the room. He had much more to do before he could rest easy. As he reached the door of the inn, he saw two of the Cardinal's Guards waiting to take Milady to the harbour. "Gentlemen, the lady will be with you shortly. The Cardinal has asked me to tell you'll that she should be taken to her ship at the earliest and make sure that she says nothing, or no one even talks to her till the time she is sailing for England." The two Guards acknowledged Athos' message and Athos was soon on his way back to La Rochelle.

Reaching the camp, he saw Porthos and Aramis with D'artagnan who had just come off duty. Without wasting any time, Athos told his friends all that had happened.

"This is terrible. We must reach the Duke before Milady can carry out her evil scheme," declared D'artagnan with a sense of urgency.

But Athos replied, "You forget my friend, that we are in the middle of a war. How can we just leave our King and our duties and go across the Channel to save the enemy?"

D'artagnan smiled and said, "I wasn't suggesting that we go to England. What if we send Planchet. You know that he can be trusted."

Athos agreed to that plan and with a message from the Queen for the Duke of Buckingham, Planchet was ordered to leave for London. "We must all drink a toast to Planchet's successful mission," offered D'artagnan. "And oh, I must thank you, my friends, for sending me this excellent bottle of wine from the Inn. I see that you did not forget about me here in the trenches," said D'artagnan as he brought forth a bottle of wine.

Athos exclaimed, "We never sent you any wine!"

D'artagnan's eyebrows knit together as he tried to fathom the mystery of the wine bottle. Porthos

though poured the spirit in a glass and was about to raise it to his lips, saying, "It's a bottle of wine and it is meant to be drunk. Let's just go ahead and drink. We can solve the mystery later!"

But even as Porthos started to raise the glass, D'artagnan jumped forward and slapped the glass away from the Musketeer. Porthos looked on, dazed, as the young cadet rushed out of the tent to where a member of his company was standing. D'artagnan and the Musketeers watched in horror as they saw the man lying on the floor, dead, even as he continued foaming at his mouth.

Athos softly mumbled, "The wine was poisoned. It seems that the Cardinal has already started with his plans to kill us!"

Chapter Twelve

Murder

Even as Planchet boarded a ship for Dover from Calais, a carriage pulled in before the Duke of Buckingham's mansion in London. Aware of who was calling on him, the Duke himself arrived at the door to greet his guest.

As the Duke helped Milady get down from the carriage, she smiled and informed him, "I am here as an emissary from His Eminence, Cardinal Richelieu of France."

The Duke, too, smiled sarcastically and replied, "If he wants more diamonds for you to take back after stealing them from me, I am sorry, I will not be able to oblige!"

Milady's smile vanished from her face as she replied, "Milord, I come here on a rather serious political mission. The Cardinal wants me to advise you against sending your troops to assist the Huguenots at La Rochelle."

This amused the Duke of Buckingham even more, as he told Milady, "The Cardinal rules over France and I look after the political interests of England. His mere request will not suffice."

Milady was slightly taken aback by the Duke's bold stance and she calmy returned, "Even at the cost of the Queen's well-being and honour?"

"When King Louis XIII will not remain the King of France any longer, then how can anything happen to my dear Anne?" assured the Duke nonchalantly.

Milady realised, as she has also told the Cardinal himself earlier at the Red Dove Inn, that the Duke was not going to budge from his position of helping the Huguenots unsettle the throne of France. Therefore, without wasting any more time with words and threats, she reached into her purse

and took a revolver out of it. Pointing it towards the Duke of Buckingham, Milady courageously offered, "Then perhaps your death will prove to be some kind of a hindrance in this matter, am I right?"

But Milady had carelessly not taken into account the fact that she was indeed standing at the Duke of Buckingham's mansion in London and was not in her native land of France. Even before she had managed to point the gun at the British Prime Minister, four guards that were present with the Duke pounced on her and decapacitated her immediately.

"Ah Milady, ever so courageous but a fool at the end of it all," the Duke smilingly declared. He then turned to one of his officers and said, "Lieutenant Felton, if you may, I have a prisoner for you."

Milady looked at the Duke, astonished at his words and pleaded, "I don't think you need to arrest me. I shall just go back to the Cardinal and let him know that you will not change your plans!"

But the Duke still feigned delight at Milady's words and assured her, "You shall find our Tower of London quite like your French Bastille. There will be no need to tell the Cardinal anything, since you will remain here as our guest for quite some time now."

Then the Duke of Buckingham once again turned to his officer, Lieutenant Felton, and told him in confidence, "Beware of this woman, Felton, for she will try everything to convince you to side with her. She will plot, she will use her beauty and her many charms, she will even try to connive with you. But I am entrusting her to you, since I am confident about your loyalty to me. Do not forget that you are like my son and we have fought many battles together, we have saved each other many a time from being killed by enemy shells. Guard her with all your life, Felton, for me and for England."

"Milord, you need not have any fears. Milady will never set foot in France again, at least not till you win the war and become their new ruler," assured Felton, as a screaming and ranting Milady was taken away by the English guards.

Milady knew that she was in great misfortune and that it was not going to be easy for her to find her way out of it. Nevertheless, she decided to try and win over Lieutenant Felton's affections.

Every day, as soon as she would hear Felton's footsteps approaching her cell, she would burst into tears and fall back in deep prayer, begging the Lord to end her suffering. She had already stopped accepting any food that was given to her, pleading with her jailors instead to instead kill her and let her end the torture that she was in.

Felton, who was a deeply religious and benevolent man himself, slowly started believing Milady's play-acting and felt sorry for the poor woman. "I hear you have declined your food," he told Milady, when the jailor informed him of her refusal to eat.

"Yes, I just want to die now as soon as I can. My life is finished as it is, I cannot take this humiliation any longer. The man who took me away from my

family when I was just a little girl, who abused me, who mistreated me, I will not let him be my executioner. I have not been able to exact revenge yet, but I will surely not let him decide how my life ends," Milady proudly informed a bewildered Felton.

"What are you saying? Are you suggesting that the Duke of Buckingham is responsible for your doom?" asked Felton, trying to confirm his worst fears.

Milady sensed that Felton was already caught in the web of her charms and went on, "Oh, you will not understand my plight. After all, you have pledged your loyalty to him. Leave me alone please, let me at least suffer in peace!" and Milady retreated into a corner, falling back to her prayer.

Felton could only feel the greatest sorrow for her. Milady's entire act against the Duke of Buckingham had greatly influenced Felton's loyalties. He was now of the opinion that the Duke was indeed a rotten human being. He had made up his mind — he was going to save Milady's honour and avenge her misery!

The next morning, Felton burst into Milady's prison cell and, grabbing her by her shoulders, said, "It is time for you to go back home. Come with me. Be quiet, but move fast before the others are alerted!"

Milady tried to hide her joy at the turn of events, but she still had a job to do. She burst into tears and holding Felton's hands, she fell to his knees crying, "But what of that scoundrel of a man? He will once again go free, perhaps only to find someone else like me and make a monster out of her too! I am grateful to you for helping me like this, but no, I cannot leave for France... not until I make sure that the Duke of Buckingham is dealt with forever!"

Felton almost felt the shame that Milady was apparently suffering and he assured her, "My first task is to get you away from here. But do not worry! I shall also take care of the Duke and then join you to go with you to France!"

So saying, Felton led Milady through an intricate maze of corridors which took them out the rear end of the Tower of London. Soon, they were making

their way down the side of a rocky mountain cliff, until they reached a boat that was tied to a huge rock.

Felton helped Milady get into the boat and then rowed towards a sloop that was waiting for them at a distance. As Milady boarded the marine ship, he said, "I have made an arrangement with the master of this boat. He will take us to France from here. You should take some rest here, while I go and settle scores with our enemy. Fear not, my love, for you shall soon be rid of your gory past and we will live our lives happily in France in a few days' time!" Thus, kissing Milady on her forehead, Felton started rowing back vigourously towards land.

The Duke of Buckingham was in the process of launching his battleships across the English Channel to aid the Huguenots in their struggles against the King's armies. The British troops were moving according to their filed ranks at the harbour when Lieutenant Felton arrived there, ready to carry out his mission for the love of his life.

Felton scanned the crowd that had gathered there and spotted the Duke of Buckingham on one of his ships, standing along with the ministers of King Charles' court. Clutching the knife that he had hidden within his overcoat, Felton started walking in the direction of the English Prime Minister.

As he steered through the crowd that had gathered at the harbour, Felton brushed against a thin, plain looking man and as they both stumbled, the man apologised, "Pardon, Monsieur!" But Felton did not even hear Planchet say anything. Instead, he tightened his grip on the knife and started walking faster towards the Duke. Felton's suspicious actions did not go unnoticed by Planchet and, fearing something foul, the Frenchman too started running towards the Duke to warn him of the threat to his life.

But as Planchet got caught up in the bustling crowd, Lieutenant Felton reached by the Duke's side and even as the Duke turned to him and flashed a warm smile, the young officer of the Duke's retinue, pulled out his knife and plunged it right into the Duke of Buckingham's heart. "Milady, this one is for you," were the only words that he cried out.

The soldiers who had gathered around the staggering Duke of Buckingham immediately jumped forward and grabbed Felton, pushing him to the ground as they secured him. The crowd started running in all directions, even as the Duke was being attented to.

But it was all too late. Planchet could only watch in horror as the Duke of Buckingham fell back, dead.

Lieutenant Felton was being dragged away by the soldiers and as he tried to break free of their hold, he caught a glimpse of a sloop chopping away through the rough waves of the English Channel in the distance. The woman he had killed the Duke of Buckingham for, the woman he loved more than his life, had not even bothered waiting for him. Lieutenant Felton knew that he had been manipulated by the scheming French spy. He stopped resisting the guards, accepting what fate had in store for him.

Chapter Thirteen

Murder in the House of God

Cardinal Richelieu was summoned to his offices outside the walled city of La Rochelle. A messenger had just brought in a letter for him, claiming that the person who had sent it to him had mentioned it to be urgent. As the Cardinal flipped through the contents of the message, a wry smile broke out on his lips.

"The Duke of Buckingham now forever rests in England. Awaiting further orders from you at Calais. Spending the night at our usual inn. Milady."

The Cardinal relished this information for a while longer as he read and re-read the message just to satisfy himself completely. He then continued with his other plans.

The next day, a tall, dark nobleman made his way into the inn where Milady had been staying. As the blonde spy opened the door to let Count Rochefort inside, she asked at once, "So, the Cardinal is pleased with my success in England?"

"Oh yes, very much. He can now finally stop worrying about that scheming Buckingham's notorious plans," replied a smiling Rochefort.

Milady too smiled on hearing the Count's words, but immediately added, "I have done all that the Cardinal had asked me to do. Now I think it is time for me to attend to my own problems. Has the Cardinal been able to discover where Madame Bonacieux is residing?"

"You know the Cardinal, he always finds out what he needs to know. The Queen has placed Constance Bonacieux in the convent at Bethune. We need to start our journey to get there at once!"

The two of them were soon seated in the carriage. Count Rochefort put his head out of the window and hailed the driver, "To Bethune. We must reach the convent there as soon as possible!"

Little did Count Rochefort or Milady realise that he had been overheard by a small, thin man who was just about to enter the inn after his ship docked at Calais. The young man was quite alarmed to hear those words and decided that he would have to reach his master at once to inform him about this latest development. Planchet hired a horse at once and sped towards La Rochelle, to find D'artagnan.

Planchet arrived at La Rochelle amidst joyous celebrations. D'artagnan received Planchet with great joy as he declared, "You come during a time of good news, my dear friend. La Rochelle is ours!"

But Planchet gravely stared at D'artagnan and replied, "I must then ask for your forgiveness for being the bearer of such unfortunate news. The Duke of Buckingham is no more!"

D'artagnan's eyes almost fell out of their sockets as he heard those last few words, but he composed himself and said, "It is sad news no doubt. That fiendish woman seems to stop at nothing. However, the Duke was still my enemy, and I am not that devastated. Had this been news of my dear Constance..."

"But it is," Planchet interrupted, going on to tell D'artagnan all that had happened since he had arrived on the soil of France. D'artagnan's expression changed to one of fear and shock. "Quick, there is no time to lose. Find Athos, Porthos and Aramis, and we shall leave at once for Bethune."

While the Musketeers were beginning their journey, there was a knock on the doors of the convent at Bethune. A nun opened the heavy doors and stared at the beautiful blonde lady standing before her. "Yes, how can I help you?"

"I am here on the orders of His Eminence, Cardinal Richelieu, for Constance Bonacieux!" Milady replied with a smile on her lips.

"Ah!" exclaimed the nun, "It is so good that you have finally arrived. Poor Constance has been feeling rather lonely of late and she will be very happy to enjoy your company. Please go right ahead, she stays in the room at the top." And Milady followed the directions the nun gave her.

Constance was lost deep in prayer when Milady entered the room. "My dear Madame Bonacieux, it is so good to finally meet you. Why, you look just like he described you to me," Milady declared as Constance opened her eyes.

"I am sorry, I do not understand. Who is it that you are talking of?" she asked stupefied.

Milady pretended to look aghast and replied, "But why, I speak of D'artagnan of course! He, too, is on his way to take you from here. He sent me here ahead, so that I could get you ready to leave with him at once."

"D'artagnan is coming?" Constance asked, hardly able to contain her excitement. "Oh, I have dreamed of this moment for so long!"

Milady smiled, thinking of what she actually had in store for Constance, and replied, "Well then, we must start making our preparations at once. But first, we must have something to eat!"

Milady quickly organised for some food and wine and poured Constance a glass to drink. The poor girl was completely oblivious to the fact that

Milady had slipped a powdered substance into her drink. Raising her own glass, Milady joyously declared, "Raise your glass, my dear, and drink a toast with me."

Poor Constance was too excited to even consider that something could be wrong. She merely followed Milady's lead and pushed the glass back, drinking all the wine in one go.

As Constance put the glass back down on the table, the sounds of horses galloping could be heard at a distance. Constance knew that it was D'artagnan approaching the convent and rushed to the window at once to catch a sight of her beloved.

But she had only taken the first few steps when she staggered and fell to the ground. She could not manage to stand up again and started to froth at the mouth. Milady instead, rushed to the window and spied the plumed hats and red cloaks of the Musketeers. "These Musketeers just have to ruin all my plans," she muttered to herself in disgust. Picking up her belongings, Milady rushed off from there at once.

D'artagnan and the Three Musketeers tore through the convent and rushed up to Constance's quarters after being directed by a nun. D'artagnan screamed in horror as he saw Constance lying dead on the floor. Porthos alerted the nuns at the convent and Aramis rushed to get some water for the poisoned lady as D'artagnan lifted Constance in his arms and tried his best to revive her.

Athos picked up the glass which was lying on the table and looked at it carefully. He spotted the sediments of the powder that Milady had poured into Constance's drink. Putting it down gently, Athos whispered to himself, "God, this was your house and you allowed that shrew to take such a devoted and pious life so easily?"

Walking across to the young cadet, Athos placed his hands on D'artagnan's shoulders and tried to console him. The poor boy was in tears as he clutched the lifeless body of Constance close to his heart. Athos softly spoke into his ear, "D'artagnan, you can do little by crying over the dead. But you can still draw your sword and punish those who did this to her!"

D'artagnan seemed to understand Athos' words and was roused to action. "You're right, my friend. I will not let this tragedy pass by. I will see to the end of this. Milady and Rochefort must pay for their sins!"

"You take on Count Rochefort. I will deal with Milady myself. That is the least a husband owes his wife," Athos declared, his face twitching with anger. Both Porthos and Aramis stared at Athos, unable to make any sense of their friend's words. Only D'artagnan, who knew the entire story of Athos' past, nodded in acknowledgement.

At the entrance of the convent, the young cadet could see a carriage still standing there. As he rushed towards it, he saw the dark overcoat of Count Rochefort glistening inside the carriage and he lunged forward, grabbing Rochefort's cloak. "I have had enough of you... it is now time to say your last prayers!" and so saying, D'artagnan pulled the Count of the carriage and threw him with great force to the ground.

As the two clashed swords, the entire world seemed just to stop and stare at the two fighters.

Neither of them were in any mood to concede defeat and fought each other like lions. They carried on fighting through the convent, and were soon back in the courtyard where Rochefort's sword ran through D'artagnan's chest. However, even such a grievous injury was not enough to stop the young Gascon.

Finally, Count Rochefort missed his footing and slipped to the ground, as D'artagnan rushed forward and drove his sword through Rochefort's heart. The Count tried to get up again and resume the fight, but the blood kept flowing from his body and he soon slumped to the ground, dead!

Milady, who had been watching the two men fight all along from a corner, decided to use the distraction caused by Rochefort's death to escape. She managed to run towards the carriage, but just as she was about to get in, she felt the cold steel pierce through her back. A shiver ran up her spine as she heard the words, "I had warned you... Harm D'artagnan and I will make sure that this time you do not cheat death!" Athos had finally avenged himself on Milady.

Chapter Fourteen

Killing the Dead

Athos first bound Milady securely, making sure that the Cardinal's fiendish spy could not find any way to escape the Musketeers. Placing her in the carriage, Athos turned to his friends and said, "I have some work to finish before we can all deal with this woman. I shall be back as soon as I can. In the meantime, I want you to stand guard here and make sure she does not escape. There is no saying what she will do if she manages to escape this time as well." Porthos, Aramis and D'artagnan stared at Athos, but neither of them dared to interject.

As promised, Athos came back in a short while. He was accompanied by a large man, who had a red cloak tied to his back and had his face covered

in a black mask. The Musketeers and D'artagnan understood at once that Athos had gone to employ the services of an executioner to deal with Milady.

Athos instructed his friends to follow the two of them with the carriage until the coast, which was located a little distance away from Bethune. Everyone remained silent, until they all reached a deserted spot on the coastline.

Athos then walked up to the carriage and dragged Milady out of there and threw her on her knees. The evil woman screamed, "How dare you arrest me? Do you know what will happen to you when I speak about your actions to the Cardinal?"

Athos stared right into Milady's eyes, silencing her at once. "Now that we are all gathered here, I suggest we begin with the process. D'artagnan, we shall begin with you. Do you believe that Madame Milady de Winters had indeed done any wrong according to the laws of the land?"

D'artagnan nodded his head and replied, "She is responsible for the murder of Constance Bonacieux and for also attempting to kill me. It was she who had sent me that poisoned wine from the Red Dove Inn. Fortunately, I was saved, but a poor soldier of the King's army met his death because of her."

Porthos, too, added, "She alone is responsible for the murder of the Duke of Buckingham. He should have died honourably in battle, rather than through subterfuge."

"Not to mention the death of Lieutenant Felton. He was hung today for murdering the Duke of Buckingham, but it was she who instigated him with utter lies," Aramis declared, fuming in Milady's direction.

"And now, my friends, let me tell you about the harm she has done to me. I married her when she was just sixteen. I gave her my name, my wealth, and shared with her everything in my life. And it was only later that I discovered that she had been branded with the fleur-de-lis! The punishment for that crime is death!" Athos declared, as Porthos and Aramis stared at him. This was the first time they had learnt about Athos' past, though the close friendship of the Three Musketeers was known all over Paris.

But even as Athos finished speaking, Milady started screaming once again. "That is no reason to kill me. You do not know how and why I was branded! You cannot prove anything this way. You will first need to find the man who branded me, you will..."

"And what it that person is standing right here?" said the executioner, interrupting Milady's cries for mercy. Everybody gathered there turned to look at the executioner. Even Athos was surprised.

The executioner walked slowly towards Milady and took off his mask. The villainous woman stared at the bald headed, pale faced man, his eyes cold and hard as if they were made of stone. And then Milady let off a scream that seemed to pierce even through the heavens. "No, no, no! It cannot be, it just cannot be! Not you, not you! The Executioner of Lille! It cannot be you!"

Athos was stunned to learn of this. All he knew about the man was that he was an executioner. He had no idea that the man he had hired was actually the man who had branded Milady for her terrible crimes against the Church.

The Executioner of Lille began by saying, "This woman here was once in training to become a nun. But the evil that she possessed in her heart helped her to decieve the priest who was training her in the affairs of the Church. She managed to convince him to run away with her and start a new life together. Since they had no money of their own, she got him to steal valuables from the Church. Eventually they were both arrested. That man was my brother!"

"She then managed to trap her jailer using her charms and escaped from Lille. My brother was convicted of his crimes and by law, was to be branded with the fleur-de-lis, and it was my job, as the executioner of the town, to brand my own brother a thief! He, too, was sentenced to ten years in prison, but managed to escape and joined this woman. During this time, living with the shame of having branded my own brother, I had managed to find her and branded her with the fleur-de-lis

as well, seeking some redemption for my brother. When they were reunited, they ran away to a small village, where they began their lives again as brother and sister. I had to suffer for his crime of escaping prison, and was sentenced to complete his term," continued the Executioner of Lille.

The executioner then turned towards Athos and said, "But the list of this woman's misdeeds had only just began. It was in this village that she seduced the lord of the province and he married her, making her the rich Countess de la Fere. My brother, on realising that she had never loved him to begin with, went back to Lille to nurse his broken heart back. It was there that he got to know of the predicament I was in because of his escape from prison. Unable to bear the shame, he gave himself up to the authorities, allowing me to become a free man once again. That night, he killed himself in his cell."

Holding Milady by the back of her neck, the Executioner of Lille declared, "She is responsible for many crimes committed against the Church and also for the death of my brother. I would therefore ask you gentlemen for your verdict. Is she guilty, or innocent?"

D'artagnan, Porthos and Aramis cried "Guilty" together. So did Athos and the Executioner of Lille after a short pause.

As Milady continued to scream and struggle, the executioner pushed her into a boat that had been tied to the rocks on the shore and started rowing towards the other side. Milady's screams curdled everyone's blood and D'artagnan started to slowly press forward, considering saving Milady from her death.

But as he reached the waves, Athos grabbed him by his arm and very slowly said, "If you fall to her charms this time, my friend, my sword will put you to the ground forever."

As soon as they reached the land on the other side, the Executioner of Lille pushed Milady to her knees and took out his long, heavy sword. Despite Milady's desperate howls, he brought his sword down on her and killed her. There was silence all across the shoreline.

The man then spread his red cloak on the ground and wrapped Milady's lifeless body into it. He carefully put back the corpse in the boat and rowed to the center of the sea, where he dropped the blood stained cloak into the water, praying, "May God finally have some mercy on her soul!"

The Three Musketeers and D'artagnan took their hats off as well, paying obeisance to the departed.

Chapter Fifteen

One for All, and
All for One!

As the Three Musketeers and D'artagnan crossed the gates of Paris, they found the entire city celebrating the tremendous victory at La Rochelle. The four friends, too, joined in the thrill, as they slowly made their way towards the palace, to unite with the rest of their companies.

However, no sooner did they arrive at the King's residence, than they were confronted by four soldiers sent by the Cardinal. "Monsieur D'artagnan!" called out one of them, "You are under arrest. I charge you with murder of a public servant. You need to come with me to His Eminence, the Cardinal at once!"

D'artagnan was well aware of Cardinal Richelieu's powers and he shot a troubled look at Athos. The Musketeer however, remained calm and said, "There is no need to panic. Come, we shall all accompany you to the Cardinal!"

As they finally reached the Cardinal's offices, the officer who had arrested D'artagnan asked the young Gascon to go into another room. And just as the Three Musketeers tried to follow their friend, they were stopped by the Cardinal's Guards, as one of them said, "I am sorry, but the Cardinal would like to meet the accused in private." Athos turned to D'artagnan and said rather loudly, so that the Cardinal himself could hear him, "Go ahead, my friend! The three of us shall wait for you here."

D'artagnan walked into a large room. A long table was present right at the center of the hall and on the other side of it stood a man in a red cloak. It was Cardinal Richelieu, the most powerful man in the whole of France. D'artagnan gulped, trying to steady his nerves.

The Cardinal got up from his seat slowly and walked over to D'artagnan. With a smile, he declared, "Ah, my young friend! If fate had willed otherwise, you and I would have been friends. But alas, you had long ago decided to work against me. And finally, you have murdered two of my most able workers, people who have done all they could for France at my behest!"

D'artagnan tried to look defiant and said, "And yet, they were murderers and finally got the justice they deserved."

The Cardinal was a little taken aback by D'artagnan's tone and replied, "Milady, and Rochefort too... I must say you have come quite a long way from just being a cadet in the King's corps. Now you must pay for all that you have done with your own life."

D'artagnan shivered as he realised that his end was perhaps near. But suddenly he remembered the piece of paper that Athos had shoved into his hands as they had started walking towards the Cardinal's residence. He remembered Athos saying, "Don't be afraid of anything that he says.

If he threatens you needlessly, then just show him this parchment."

D'artagnan fumbled through the pockets of his overcoat and taking out the piece of parchment, said, "I respectfully submit to your Eminence, that you please look through the contents of this before committing me to my sentence."

The Cardinal snatched the parchment from D'artagnan's hand and read it out aloud. It was only after he had gone through the first line that he realised what had happened. The parchment read, "The bearer of this letter works under my command and whatever he or she may have done is for the good of France, so let him or her continue in their duties. December, 1627. Cardinal Richelieu."

D'artagnan, who, too, had heard the message on the parchment for the first time, felt a wave of relief. Athos had saved him from harm yet again! The Cardinal was at a loss for words as he shifted about nervously with the paper in his hand.

After a few moments of silence, the royal pontiff tore the paper into smithereens and without uttering another word, started writing another

note. D'artagnan stared in horror at the strewn pieces of paper, as he muttered to himself, "Is he now writing my death sentence? Oh, what have I done?"

Having finished writing, the Cardinal walked back to where D'artagnan was standing and held out the paper before the young cadet. D'artagnan read through the note at once and was left standing in a state of complete shock.

He finally found his voice again, as he said, "Your Eminence, I do not deserve this... you want to appoint me as a Lieutenant in the King's Musketeers? No, Monseigneur, I cannot accept. But I have three friends, who are way more superior than I am and deserve this post much more than I do!"

The Cardinal waved his hands, dismissing D'artagnan and added, "It is to you that I give this certificate, and now it is for you to decide what you want to do with it."

D'artagnan stood there in silence for quite some time, and finally started walking to where his friends were impatiently standing for him. Athos rushed to him at once, and asked, "Why do you look so pale? What happened in there?"

D'artaganan handed the parchment to Athos and said, "This belongs to you my friend! You deserve this much more than I ever can!"

Athos quickly glanced through the Cardinal's writing and replied with a smile, "Me? A Lieutenant? Oh come now, my young friend! Musketeer Athos is too small to accept such a honourable post and the Count de la Fere might be insulted!" Athos' eyes twinkled as he tried to surpress his laughter.

D'artagnan, too, smiled at his friend's words and turning to Porthos, said, "I think that you should accept this!" But Porthos good naturedly replied, "And not marry my Duchess? I won't be wearing the uniform for much longer, D'artagnan, and therefore, you should take this yourself!"

D'artagnan was still not willing to take the job, and he turned to Aramis and said, "You, Aramis, are so learned and wise. You will surely make a fine Lieutenant!"

Aramis smiled and replied, "I think I will make a much better priest that a Lieutenant, my friend! I intend to live my dream soon enough and this title will be completely wasted on me."

D'artagnan looked confused as Athos wrote D'artagnan's name on the parchment and handed it back to him. The young Gascon sadly declared, "But as an officer I will not be able to find any time to spend with you, my friends! What is the point then, of being a lieutenant?"

Athos smiled and replied, "Is that all? In which case you should remember, that we are now the Four Musketeers, and no piece of paper can change that."

Porthos and Aramis then joined Athos in taking out their swords and, bringing them all together, the Four Musketeers joyously sang, "One for all, and all for one!"

About the Author

▪ Alexandre Dumas

Alexandre Dumas, the author of *The Three Musketeers,* was born on July 24, 1802, in Villiers-Cotterets, Aisne, France. His father, a general in the French army, died when he was four years old, making it hard for the family to make ends meet.

Dumas started out writing historical plays and musical comedies and, though they were not his best works, his striking imaginative ability, wit and intelligence stood out quite clearly. The period after the revolution of 1830 in France was quite unproductive for Dumas, as the new king did not see eye to eye with him. He was, thus, in exile for a while, during which he wrote a series of light-hearted travel books.

It was only after his return to Paris that Dumas began writing novels, and *The Three Musketeers* (1844), *The Count of Monte Cristo* (1846) and *The Vicomte de Bragelonne* (1850) were all written during this phase of his career. Along with just being gripping plots in themselves, these works also offer a valuable insider's perspective on the political scenario of France in the 17th century.

Despite his success and aristocratic connections, Dumas was frequently in debt as a result of spending lavishly. The large and costly Chateau de Monte Cristo that he built was often filled with strangers and acquaintances who took advantage of his eagerness to indulge. In his later years, mainly out of desperation to pay his creditors, Dumas produced a number of works of poor quality which were commercially not very successful. His son, Alexandre, and his daughter, Madame Petel, were his foremost source of hope and joy in his last days, and he died in poverty on December 5, 1870.

▪ Characters

D'artagnan: The protagonist of the novel, D'artagnan is an ambitious young man from Gascon whose life's ambition is to join the King's Three Musketeers. Noble and honourable, but crafty when needed, he is not afraid to face all challenges that lie in his path once he sets his mind to something.

Athos: The oldest and most important of the Three Musketeers, Athos is the closest to D'artagnan. A refined aristocrat, he is the maturest of the four friends and his wise decisions at the right time save them from many a trouble; yet he has something in his heart that disturbs him deeply.

Aramis: One of the Three Musketeers, Aramis is a handsome, usually quiet young man, who claims that his true calling is to become a priest.

Porthos: One of the Three Musketeers, he seems to be the most loud, brash, and impulsive of the lot. Nonetheless, he is a loyal friend and a courageous fighter.

Milady de Winter: An extremely beautiful but dangerous and cunning woman who works as the Cardinal's spy. Her sly contrivances are responsible for many a death in the novel.

Constance Bonacieux: A young woman married to a petty old man, Constance is one of the Queen's attendants. She plays an important role in protecting the Queen's reputation from being scarred by the Cardinal's designs and eventually falls in love with D'artagnan.

Monsieur Bonacieux: A pompous fool who does not respect his wife, Constance. His fear and gullibility are easily manipulated by the Cardinal to get him to spy on her.

Monsieur de Tréville: The competent Captain of the King's Musketeers, and also an old friend of D'artagnan's father.

King Louis XIII: The ineffective King of France who relies largely on Cardinal Richelieu to run his kingdom.

Cardinal Richelieu: The King's most prominent advisor, the Cardinal is unanimously recognised as the most powerful man in France. Ruthlessly selfish, he is also an efficient administrator who works towards maintaining the reputation of the king, as on it is based his own standing.

Queen Anne: The Queen of France, a lady of Spanish origin. She does not share a relationship of love with her husband, and actually holds the Duke of Buckingham dear to her heart.

Duke of Buckingham: The most powerful man in England after its King, the Duke of Buckingham is deeply in love with Queen Anne of France. An enemy of the Cardinal, one of the reasons he is adamant on England's war against France is that a victory would get him closer to his love.

Count Rochefort: One of the Cardinal's dangerous spies, often referred to as the man with a black patch over one of his eyes and a scar on his cheek.

Kitty: Milady's maid who falls in love with D'artagnan and informs him about her mistress' wicked plans.

Planchet: D'artagnan's reliable and brave manservant.

■ Questions

Chapter 1
- *Who was the young man from Gascony and why was he on his way to France?*
- *Why did D'artagnan get into a fight at the inn in Meung?*
- *What did D'artagnan see when he woke up after his injury and looked out of the window?*

Chapter 2
- *Name the Captain and the King's Three Musketeers?*
- *In his meeting with the Captain, what difficulty does D'artagnan face in becoming part of the King's Musketeers?*

Chapter 3
- *Briefly describe how D'artagnan unintentionally ends up offending all the Three Musketeers.*
- *How does he manage to get out of the above situation?*

Chapter 4
- *What was Monsieur Bonacieux's relationship to D'artagnan?*
- *What was the name of Monsieur Bonacieux's wife?*
- *Why does D'artagnan not stop the Cardinal's guards from arresting Monsieur Bonacieux?*
- *What revelations are made in this chapter about Queen Anne's private life and Cardinal Richelieu?*

Chapter 5
- *Why does D'artagnan agree to help Constance save the Queen from trouble?*
- *Whom does D'artagnan confront out of jealousy when he sees him with Constance?*
- *What does the Queen gift her lover as a token of remembrance?*

Chapter 6
- *What is Bastille?*

- *What exciting news does Rochefort bring the Cardinal?*
- *What conclusions can you draw about the character of Bonacieux from the events in this chapter?*

Chapter 7
- *Briefly describe Cardinal Richelieu's scheme to disgrace the Queen.*

Chapter 8
- *Whom does D'artagnan see entering the house when hiding in another room with Constance?*
- *What obstacles does the Cardinal have in store for the Three Musketeers and D'artagnan?*

Chapter 9
- *How is the Cardinal's plan to embarrass the Queen foiled?*
- *What does the Queen gift D'artagnan for helping protect her from being ashamed?*

Chapter 10
- *What happens to D'artagnan while on his way to meet Constance?*
- *What is the story of Athos' past?*
- *Who warns D'artagnan of Milady's evil intentions and why?*
- *What is the fleur-de-lis?*

Chapter 11
- *Name the two major groups into which the population of France was divided?*
- *Where do the Three Musketeers decide to take some rest during the siege of La Rochelle?*
- *Why does the Cardinal want to send Milady to the Duke of Buckingham?*
- *Briefly describe Athos' confrontation with Milady.*
- *What is the story behind the wine bottle gifted to Athos?*

Chapter 12
- *What mistake does Milady make for her to get arrested?*
- *Name the officer in charge of not letting Milady escape at any cost.*

- *What circumstances lead to the death of the Duke of Buckingham?*

Chapter 13
- *Who overhears the conversation between Milady and Count Rochefort?*
- *How does Milady avenge herself on Constance?*

Chapter 14
- *Who is the executioner Athos brings with him?*

Chapter 15
- *What is the slogan the Three Musketeers are so fond of?*
- *How does D'artagnan manage to escape the Cardinal's wrath?*
- *What position is D'artagnan offered by the Cardinal and how does he react to this offer?*